"I wanted you to come to the ranch so I could spend more time with you."

Emily opened her mouth to say something, but Sloan held up his hand.

"I wanted to spend more time with you because I'm attracted to you."

She stared up at him. "You're attracted to me?"

"Well, you don't have to look so damned unhappy about it."

"No," she said, her mind whirling. "No, actually, I think I'm flattered."

"Funny. You look scared to death."

Dear Reader,

Well, June may be the traditional month for weddings, but we here at Silhouette find June is busting out all over—with babies! We begin with Christine Rimmer's *Fifty Ways To Say I'm Pregnant.* When bound-for-the-big-city Starr Bravo shares a night of passion with the rancher she's always loved, she finds herself in the family way. But how to tell him? *Fifty Ways* is a continuation of Christine's Bravo Family saga, so look for the BRAVO FAMILY TIES flash. And for those of you who remember Christine's JONES GANG series, you'll be delighted with the cameo appearance of an old friend....

Next, Joan Elliott Pickart continues her miniseries THE BABY BET: MACALLISTER'S GIFTS with *Accidental Family,* the story of a day-care center worker and a single dad with amnesia who find themselves falling for each other as she cares for their children together. And there's another CAVANAUGH JUSTICE offering in Special Edition from Marie Ferrarella: in *Cavanaugh's Woman,* an actress researching a film role needs a top cop—and Shaw Cavanaugh fits the bill nicely. *Hot August Nights* by Christine Flynn continues THE KENDRICKS OF CAMELOT miniseries, in which the reserved, poised Kendrick daughter finds her one-night stand with the town playboy coming back to haunt her in a big way. Janis Reams Hudson begins MEN OF CHEROKEE ROSE with *The Daddy Survey,* in which two little girls go all out to get their mother a new husband. And don't miss *One Perfect Man,* in which almost-new author Lynda Sandoval tells the story of a career-minded events planner who has never had time for romance until she gets roped into planning a party for the daughter of a devastatingly handsome single father. So enjoy the rising temperatures, all six of these wonderful romances...and don't forget to come back next month for six more, in Silhouette Special Edition.

Happy Reading!

Gail Chasan
Senior Editor

The Daddy Survey

JANIS REAMS HUDSON

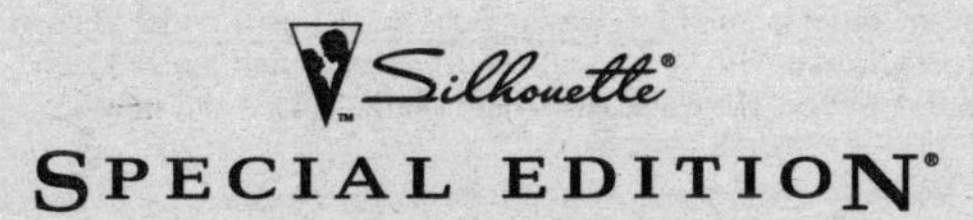

Published by Silhouette Books
America's Publisher of Contemporary Romance

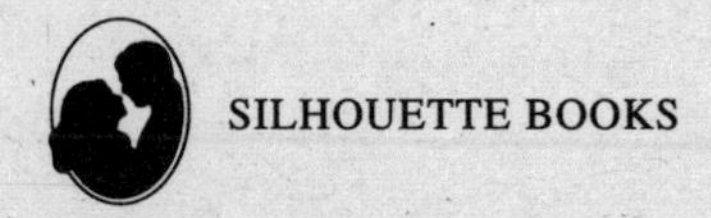

ISBN 0-373-24619-6

THE DADDY SURVEY

This edition published by arrangement with Harlequin Books S.A.

Visit Silhouette Books at www.eHarlequin.com

Printed in U.S.A.

Books by Janis Reams Hudson

Silhouette Special Edition

Resist Me if You Can #1037
The Mother of His Son #1095
His Daughter's Laughter #1105
Until You #1210
**Their Other Mother* #1267
**The Price of Honor* #1332
**A Child on the Way* #1349
**Daughter on His Doorstep* #1434
**The Last Wilder* #1474
†*The Daddy Survey* #1619

*Wilders of Wyatt County
†Men of the Cherokee Rose

JANIS REAMS HUDSON

was born in California, grew up in Colorado, lived in Texas for a few years and now calls central Oklahoma home. She is the author of more than twenty-five novels, both contemporary and historical romances. Her books have appeared on the Waldenbooks, B. Dalton and Bookrak bestseller lists and earned numerous awards, including the National Reader's Choice Award and Reviewer's Choice awards from *Romantic Times*. She is a three-time finalist for the coveted RITA® Award from Romance Writers of America and is a past president of RWA.

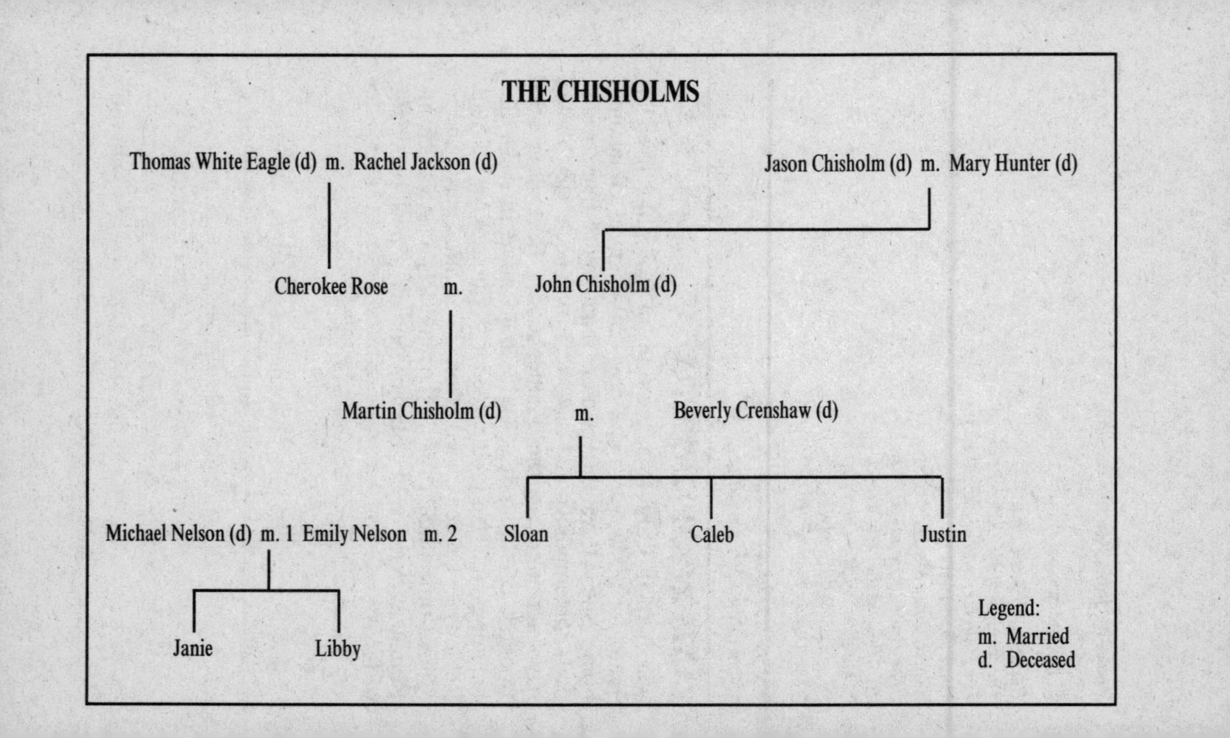
THE CHISHOLMS
Thomas White Eagle (d) m. Rachel Jackson (d)
Jason Chisholm (d) m. Mary Hunter (d)
Cherokee Rose m. John Chisholm (d)
Martin Chisholm (d) m. Beverly Crenshaw (d)
Michael Nelson (d) m. 1 Emily Nelson m. 2
Sloan
Caleb
Justin
Janie
Libby
Legend:
m. Married
d. Deceased

Chapter One

When Sloan Chisholm pulled up across the street from the roadside café, thoughts of a chicken fried steak loomed paramount in his mind. He wanted a big one. Big enough to hang off the sides of the platter, with a whopping pile of mashed potatoes on the side, and both buried under at least an inch of thick, creamy-white gravy. He hadn't had a chicken fry since a week ago Saturday, and he thought he might be suffering the early stages of withdrawal. It was time for a fix.

Before he got the chance to harden his arteries, however, he ran smack into something that would change his life forever: The Daddy Survey.

Actually, his life changed a couple of minutes before that, after he checked on the horse he was trailering and then crossed the street, stepped through the door of the café, and fell head over heels in love.

Sloan had managed to live thirty-five years without falling in love. Not really. Not bone-deep, gut-clenching, breath-stealing love. Those other two times didn't count.

Funny, but even with all of his grandmother's recent grumblings about wanting him and his two brothers to get married so she could spoil a batch of great-grandchildren, Sloan had never really expected his heart to take that slow, sweet slide into helpless delight. But he could feel it happening inside him now, and it stunned him. And even supposing that he had expected to fall in love, he sure never would have thought he'd be the type of man to fall for two females at once, but there was no help for it. There they stood, and he was a goner.

They were the most adorable creatures Sloan had ever seen. Both were blond, although one's hair was a shade or two darker than the other's. Both had blue eyes and enough similar facial features to have him guessing they were sisters, but one had dimples and the other didn't. One wore glasses, one didn't. One was taller than the other.

One was eight, the other about six.

"Good afternoon, sir." The oldest of the two girls pushed her wire-rimmed glasses up on the bridge of her pert little nose. She hugged a stack of menus and a notebook to her chest, with the eraser end of a pencil sticking up out of the notebook's wire spirals. Behind the lenses of her glasses, her sky-blue eyes studied him closely. "Smoking or non?"

"That's nonsmoking," the little one clarified.

The elder frowned at her. "He knows what *non* means."

The younger merely flashed her dimples.

Before an argument could break out—not that one appeared imminent, but Sloan wasn't taking any chances—he slapped a hand to his shirt pocket. It was just as empty of cigarettes as it had been for the past year and a half. And he was just as surprised by it now as when he'd first quit. "Non, please, ladies," he offered with a sweep of his hat.

They led him to a booth next to the wide front window.

Sloan had dined in fancier establishments, but he'd also eaten in worse. This one ranked somewhere below average. The red vinyl of his seat bore a split from front to back wide enough to show the white stuffing inside. A few feet from his table the worn carpeting curled up where the seam connecting two pieces was coming apart, ready to trip some unsuspecting customer or waitress and trigger a lawsuit.

But the table was clean, and the staff, so far, was adorable.

An instant later, when the waitress approached with a plastic tumbler of ice water, Sloan got his second kick in the gut. She wasn't beautiful, in the movie-star sense of the word, but she was so damn pretty she nearly took his breath away.

Dainty was the word that came to mind. Or maybe *delicate.* Not that either was a word Sloan had much experience with, considering he spent most of his time with cattle, horses and grown men who usually reeked of barnyard sweat. But the waitress was slightly built, and her short hair left her neck bare and looking vulnerable.

Even her eyes, the same pale yet vibrant blue as the little girls', spoke of vulnerability.

The urge to protect her startled him. Sloan wanted,

unreasonably, to take her in his arms and shield her, protect her from harm, from cold, from fear. And most of all, he realized when he saw the pale strip of skin where a ring had once been—but was no longer—on the fourth finger of her left hand, he wanted, desperately, to protect her from ever having to sleep alone again.

He wanted to protect her from guys like him.

Her smile was polite and friendly without being overly so. She placed the water before him. "I'll give you a minute to look over the menu and decide what you want. Girls," she said to the two little beauties, "you know you're not supposed to bother the customers."

"But, Mother—"

"They're not bothering me," Sloan claimed, interrupting whatever the oldest girl had been about to say. "In fact, I can't remember when I've enjoyed prettier company."

The youngest girl giggled and blushed; the older one smiled shyly.

"All right, but don't make pests of yourselves," their mother warned softly.

"Yes, ma'am," they said in unison.

Sloan watched the waitress walk away, admiring the gentle sway of her hips and giving thanks for Levi Strauss and his denim tents that nobody wanted all those decades ago during the California gold rush.

"That's our mommy," the littlest girl said.

Sloan pulled his gaze back to the girls and smiled. "Yeah?"

"Uh-huh. Her name's Emily. Emily Nelson. Do you think she's pretty?"

"Yes, ma'am," he said with feeling. "I surely

do.'' Emily. Emily Nelson. ''She's every bit as pretty as the two of you.''

This was where he could logically say something stupid, like *Your daddy is one lucky man.* But that would be pumping the girls for information, and he couldn't bring himself to sink that low. Besides, if their daddy was out of the picture, mentioning him could hurt these two little innocent angels.

So, instead, he smiled and asked if they would like to join him for lunch.

''Thank you, sir,'' said the oldest one, all serious and grown-up, ''but we've already eaten.''

''That's too bad.'' And he meant it. It would be a kick to sit across the table from them for half an hour or so. Especially considering that he usually spent his days staring at the south end of a northbound steer. ''Maybe you could just keep me company while I eat?''

''Wellll...'' The older girl stole a quick glance at her sister, then looked back at him. ''We could do that, and maybe you'd like to take our survey while you wait for your order.''

''Survey, huh? What kind of survey?''

''Oops.'' The little one nudged her sister. ''Mommy's coming.'' Then, to him, ''Do you know what you want to eat yet?''

Sloan tracked the waitress's progress toward him like a starving man waiting for a feast. With a coffeepot in one hand and a pitcher of iced tea in the other, she moved like a dancer from table to table, filling a mug here, a tumbler there, with a smile, a question, a comment for each customer.

When Sloan caught himself wondering if she

moved that gracefully, smiled that beautifully, while beneath a man in bed, he forced himself to look away.

Man alive, forget about protecting her. Who was going to protect him?

She came and stood beside his table. ''Do you know what you want?''

Oh, boy, honey, he thought. *That is one loaded question.*

She must have seen something in his eyes, for she cleared her throat then blinked slowly down at her order pad and rephrased her question. ''Are you ready to order?''

Without looking at the menu, Sloan kept his gaze on her face and ordered a chicken fried steak with all the trimmings.

Without looking up at him, she scribbled on her pad and said, ''I'll get that out to you as soon as it's ready.''

She is so damn pretty, he thought again as she went to turn in his order.

''Sir?''

Sloan turned back to the girls. ''Sloan,'' he said. ''Call me Sloan.''

''Okay.'' The little one beamed. ''I'm Libby and this is my sister, Janie. Do you wanna take our survey?''

''Why not? What kind of survey is it?''

''It's a da—''

But Janie interrupted her younger sister. ''We're taking a survey of single men between the ages of twenty-one and sixty-five. Is that you?''

Hearing such grown-up language coming from such a young child made him want to smile.

"Twenty-one and sixty-five, huh? That's quite a range, but, yeah, I fit in there."

"And you're single?"

"Last time I checked."

Janie frowned.

"Yes," he clarified. "I'm single."

Her face cleared.

"Oh, goody," Libby said, grinning.

Janie cleared her throat. "Okay." She pulled the spiral notebook from her small stack of menus and flipped it open. "On a scale of one to five, with one being not at all and five being very, very much, how well do you like little girls?"

Sloan grinned widely. "That's easy. I'd have to give that one a five, if that's as high as I can go."

Libby giggled.

Janie marked his answer in her notebook, then looked at him out the corner of her eye. "On a scale of one to five, do you believe in spanking?"

Sloan's eyes widened. "Of little girls? I'd have to give that a zero. Nobody should spank little girls."

Both girls smiled hugely as Janie wrote down his answer.

"How much do you like liver and onions?" Janie asked.

"I'd have to give that a three."

"How much do you like ice cream?"

"That's a big five."

Janie paused and studied him carefully, such a serious look in those bright blue eyes. Then she took a deep breath and plunged on. "Yes or no, does Santa Claus know where you live?"

Sloan lost all urge to laugh over their cute questions. It was becoming obvious that what Libby had been about to say earlier was that this was a daddy survey. These girls were surveying café customers in search of a new daddy. The very idea broke his heart. He wanted to grab them and pull them onto his lap and hold them close and promise them—

Promise them what? That he would be their daddy?

Whoa, pal. Getting a little ahead of yourself, aren't you?

"Mr. Sloan?" Janie prodded.

"Oh, sorry. And it's not Mr., it's just Sloan."

"Oh, no," Libby said. "We have to call all grown-ups Mr. or Ms."

"It's a sign of respect," Janie said.

"It's a rule," Libby added.

"Well," Sloan said. "We wouldn't want to break any rules, so I guess you can call me Mr. Sloan. Now, where were we?"

"Santa," Libby told him.

"Oh, yeah. Well, sure. We've even got a chimney for him, and every year we put up a tree with lights and the works."

Both girls let out a big breath and grinned at each other. Then Janie got back down to business.

"One to five again. How much do you like puppies?"

"Oh, I like puppies a whole lot."

"Is that a five?" Janie asked.

"I'd have to say so. A definite five for puppies."

"What about kittens?" Libby asked.

"That's not on the survey," Janie protested.

"Well, it should be." Libby gave an emphatic nod, making her pale yellow curls bounce.

Janie frowned. "Okay, kittens. But it's not fair, because the other men didn't get to answer that one."

"Maybe we can ask them if they come back in," Libby offered.

Janie brightened. "Maybe we can."

"So, kittens?" Sloan asked, his stomach tightening at the thought of their asking these questions of every stranger who came in. "Kittens are a definite five. We have lots of kittens at our ranch."

Libby's eyes widened. "You do?"

"You have a ranch?" Janie asked in awe. "With horses and cows and everything?"

"Sure do. With horses and cows and everything." He pointed to his rig across the street. "See that pickup? It's got the name of our ranch right there on the door."

"Cherokee Rose," Janie read.

"Cherokee?" Libby's eyes nearly swallowed her face. "Are you a *Indian?*"

Janie frowned. "Not Indian, silly. Native American."

"He *is?*" Libby breathed, staring at Sloan in awe. "You *are?*"

"Indian's fine," Sloan said. "And yes, I'm part Indian."

Libby still stared at him wide-eyed. "Which part?"

Sloan couldn't help it—he broke out laughing. He was saved from having to explain anything more to Libby by the approach of her mother with his order.

Emily Nelson heard the cowboy's deep laughter long before she reached his table with his order. Whatever her daughters were saying to him, he was obviously enjoying himself.

He had a nice laugh. A nice face, too.

Well, maybe *nice* wasn't the right word for those

chiseled, coppery features, but *attractive* certainly fit. And *compelling.*

The thought startled her. She couldn't remember the last time she had even bothered to notice how a man looked. The last man—the *only* man—she had ever looked at or noticed in her entire life was Michael.

The expected ache at the thought of him came, as she knew it would. But it was a poignant ache these days, not the stabbing, crippling agony it had once been. Two years since his death, and she could now think of Michael with as much love and gratitude for the years they'd had together as regret for his loss.

He had been the love of her life, and he'd given her these two precious daughters who liked to entertain strangers while she worked to earn the money to get the three of them to a promised job in Arkansas. If her car hadn't broken down in the middle of nowhere she wouldn't have had to take this job merely to get the car fixed. If she had to pay a baby-sitter for the girls, she would never earn enough to fix the car. She was grateful her boss was so tolerant as to let the girls stay in the café while she waited tables.

"Mommy, Mommy!" Libby practically jumped up and down beside the man's table. Her voice carried clear across the dining room. "Mr. Sloan has a ranch with horses and kitties and everything and he's part Indian and he thinks you're *real* pretty."

Oh, Lord, Emily thought as fire stung her cheeks. *Please open a hole in the floor and let me fall in.*

But, as was usually the case, no convenient hole appeared. She had no chance of falling out of sight. No chance that the man wouldn't notice the heat flushing her cheeks.

He chuckled, and so did several other customers at nearby tables.

Emily's face burned hotter.

"Ladies," the man said. "I think we've embarrassed your mother."

"Did we, Mommy?" Libby asked, fighting a giggle. "Did we embarrass you?"

Deciding there was no graceful way to ignore her youngest daughter's comments, Emily rolled her eyes. "I'm usually embarrassed whenever you blab everything you know to the entire world."

"Ah, Mommy." Libby snickered. "But it was true. Wasn't it, Mr. Sloan?"

"Yes, ma'am," the man said as Emily set his plate down before him.

Emily hadn't meant to look at him again, but the good-natured laughter in his voice drew her gaze.

"Every word of it." And he winked. Not at her daughters, but at *her.*

Good grief. Did men still do that? Wink at women? It seemed more like something she would see on television rather than have it happen to her.

He'd *winked.* What was she supposed to do about it? Say thank-you? Scowl? Flutter her lashes?

What she felt like doing was joining her daughters in a decidedly childish giggle.

Good grief.

"That looks like manna from heaven," the man said of the food on his plate.

Feeling like an idiot for standing there staring at him like a schoolgirl with her first big crush, Emily hurriedly set his cutlery down in front of him. "I'll get you some more tea right away. Girls, run along now and let the man eat."

"But, Mommy," Libby cried.

"They're fine," the man said. "Really. If it's all right with you, I'd like them to stay and keep me company."

Pervert? Emily wondered, or nice man who liked children? Having no way of knowing, she opted for safety over the pleas of her daughters and a stranger. "That's very nice of you," she told him, "but they've bothered you long enough. Girls." She gave them *the look*, the one they knew not to argue with.

"Yes, ma'am," Janie nudged Libby to let her out of the booth. "G'bye, Mr. Sloan."

"G'bye, Mr. Sloan," Libby echoed.

Emily nearly rolled her eyes again at their pitiful tone of voice.

"'Bye, girls," the man answered back.

Emily followed the girls and shooed them onto the last two stools at the counter, where they would be out of everyone's way. A minute later she was back at the man's table refilling his iced tea.

Grateful for her promptness, Sloan smiled and thanked her. "Those are some great girls you've got. You must be proud of them."

"Thank you," she said with a slight smile. "I am. Can I get you anything else? Maybe a piece of apple pie for dessert? Baked fresh this morning."

"No, thanks. I'm fine."

She placed his ticket facedown on the table and left him to finish his meal. Sloan watched her walk away. She stopped at the counter and whispered something to her girls.

Her baby-sitter must be sick today, Sloan figured, so she'd had to bring the girls to work with her.

But the impression he'd gotten from the girls and their survey was that they hung out in the café a lot.

Raising kids alone was rough on anyone, man or woman. But when it was a woman doing the raising, and she looked as vulnerable and defenseless as a newborn kitten, it had to be more than rough. She couldn't make much money in a place like this. There didn't seem to be enough business for tips to be any good. Maybe she couldn't afford a baby-sitter. Maybe the girls came to work with her every day.

Would a boss allow that?

Sloan shrugged and tackled his chicken fry. It was none of his business. Emily Nelson was not a damsel in distress, and he was not her white knight.

Not that there was anything wrong with someone who needed a helping hand now and then, man or woman. And helping out someone in need, well, that was every person's responsibility, wasn't it?

Just because he'd gone a little overboard and thought he'd fallen in love a couple of times with a couple of damsels in distress—well, one of them had been in genuine need. The other had played him like a fish on a line. Taken advantage of his generous nature.

Or, as his brothers insisted, she'd merely read the word *sucker* that they swore was tattooed across his forehead when it came to women.

He didn't know why he had a thing for women in need, because if he took the time to envision himself with a wife, she would be a strong woman who could stand on her own beside him, not one who needed his help every time he turned around. Lord bless Connie Sue Walters. She should have cured him of helpless women, but, no, not him. A couple of years after that disaster, he'd fallen for someone new. Donna Daniels had only pretended to be helpless. She had turned out to be about as helpless as a she-bear. She'd had it in mind to convince him to sell his portion of the ranch and buy her a house in town so she could live in a manner to which she would like to have become accustomed.

No, sir, no more falling for the helpless act again, not for Sloan Chisholm.

It was a crying shame, he'd always thought, that he couldn't have fallen for Melanie. Melanie Pruitt lived on the ranch next to theirs. If ever there was a woman strong enough and smart enough to stand beside a man and face whatever came, it had to be Mel. She could ride and rope with the best cowboys, yet when she cleaned up and put on a dress, man, oh, man, she could render the cockiest cowboy speechless. She was a looker, Mel was, and that was a fact.

If all that wasn't enough to get Sloan's attention, she had been in love with him and in hot pursuit since she was five years old.

Why he'd never been able to return those feelings, he didn't know. But all he'd ever felt for Mel was a deep and abiding friendship. And now she was over him and thought of him as a friend. He had really missed out. He loved her, but as the little sister he'd never had, not the way a woman deserved to be loved.

Yes, sir, a crying shame that he always fell for the wrong ones.

That night as Emily tucked her daughters into the double bed next to hers in their motel room, Libby asked for the fifth time since supper, "You liked Mr. Sloan, didn't you, Mommy?"

And for the fifth time since supper, Emily replied, "He seemed like a nice enough man."

"But you like him, right?" Libby insisted.

Emily leaned down and kissed her youngest on the nose. "I don't know him well enough to say. Now, close your eyes and go to sleep. Both of you," she added with a smile for Janie.

"But, Mommy—"

Emily placed a finger over Libby's tiny lips. "Sleep."

Beneath her finger the tiny lips curved upward. "Okay. G'night, Mommy."

Following the round of good-nights came the usual requests for drinks, then back to the bathroom a few minutes later, then another round of kisses and hugs and good-nights. The ritual took an average of thirty minutes each night, and this night was no different. But finally the girls were tucked in, eyes closed, breaths deep and even with sleep.

God, but they were beautiful. They might look like her, but they had so much of their father in them. Especially Libby, with her outgoing personality and total lack of fear. Janie was quieter, more studious and sober, but had Michael's keen intelligence.

For the hundredth time Emily wondered if she was doing the right thing in taking them to Arkansas. It had seemed like her only choice two weeks ago when she'd made the decision to leave Colorado for a chance at a new job at the factory where her cousin worked in Fort Smith. After her job at the museum gift shop had been eliminated, Emily simply hadn't been able to find work that paid enough to cover groceries, rent, day care and all the other things two growing young girls needed.

"Oh, Michael," she whispered. "Am I doing the right thing?"

She often asked him questions, but he never answered. Leukemia had taken him two years ago. Her only answers these days were silence and doubt.

But she didn't have time to feel sorry for herself. She had to earn enough money to pay for the repairs on her car. With grim determination, she pulled her checkbook and wallet from her purse and began adding up her meager assets.

Today's tips had been decent, thanks in part to the man her daughters had been so enamored of. He'd been more than generous with the cash he'd left on his table.

A few more customers like him—and if her boss's wife would come home so he would keep his lecherous hands to himself—and Emily might be able to get her car fixed in another week. Maybe.

Sloan spent the night at a ranch outside Wagon Mound, New Mexico. Jeb Cotter was so glad to have his mare back, and without that nasty habit of trying to bite her rider—which Caleb and Justin had worked out of her—and without having to drive back to Oklahoma to retrieve her, that he put Sloan up in the guest room of his home rather than the bunkhouse, where visiting cowboys usually stayed.

When Sloan crawled into bed that night and closed his eyes, he saw two adorable little girls and their delicate, pretty mother. He'd thought about them the better part of the afternoon as he trailered the mare the rest of the way to her home ranch. Thought about them, worried about them.

It was that worry that had him stopping back at

that same café two days later on his way home. Ordinarily he would have taken a different route back to the Cherokee Rose; he liked to see new sights whenever he got the chance. But not this time.

They were none of his business, really, Emily Nelson and her daughters. He just wanted to look in, check up on them while he had the chance. After today he would never see them again, so what was the harm?

It was just past noon when he pulled up at the café that sat at the intersection of a state highway and a county road. This time he wasn't pulling a horse trailer, so he could have parked in front of the café, except business seemed to be brisk. There were no empty spots. He parked across the street, where he'd parked two days earlier, next to the motel entrance.

When he entered the café a moment later the bell over the door jingled. There were no little girls there to greet him. No delicate, sexy waitress wending her way between the tables.

He felt enormously let down, which told him he had placed way too much importance on a chance encounter.

Just as he was telling himself that this was for the best, that he had no business coming here today in the first place, he heard his name.

"Mr. Sloan!"

He spotted her immediately. It was the little one, Libby. With a grin and a wave she jumped off the bar stool at the counter and dashed toward him. Janie followed, a bit more sedate than her little sister.

"Mr. Sloan," Libby called again, rushing his way, curls bobbing, grin flashing. "You came ba—"

Sloan saw it all as if it happened in slow motion.

The loose edge of carpet, where a seam had come undone, caught the toe of Libby's small shoe and pitched her forward.

He cried out her name and lunged, but he knew he'd never reach her in time.

Libby pitched forward. She tried to catch herself by grabbing toward the table beside her, but all she managed to do was knock a customer's iced tea into the man's lap on her way down.

The customer, a fifty-something man in bib overalls, yelped in surprise.

But it was the sound of Libby's tiny head hitting the floor that stopped Sloan's heart. He dove for her just as she rolled and completed her somersault. Her feet whacked him in the face.

Sloan was much more concerned about the child than about the slight discomfort of a miniature sneaker or two in the eye. It took him a moment, as she was flailing around pretty good trying to right herself, but finally he had the child by the shoulders.

"Libby, are you all right?"

Big blue eyes looked up at him, wide with shock. "I fell down."

"You sure did, sweetie. Does your head hurt?"

Her bottom lip quivered; her eyes filled. "N-no."

"Are you sure, baby? You hit the floor pretty hard."

She sniffed and rubbed the top of her head. "I'm okay, Mr. Sloan, honest."

Sloan quickly felt her head, her arms and legs. Finding nothing broken, he let out a huge sigh of relief. It could have been worse. It could have been disastrous. But little Libby was lucky. He would be, too, he thought ruefully, if he didn't end up with two black eyes. But as long as Libby was all right, he would gladly bear the bruises.

He was helping Libby to her feet and Janie was rushing up to check on her sister when the swinging door to the kitchen crashed open and banged against the wall. A short, balding man shaped like a barrel, with a dish towel tied around his ample waist, charged out from the kitchen a half second before the door swung shut again. He brandished a stainless-steel spatula in one beefy paw. "What in blue blazes is going on out here? What have those brats done now?"

At Sloan's side, Libby whimpered.

Sloan felt steam bubble in his ears. He placed a hand on Libby's shoulder and stepped in front of her. "She's just fine. Thanks for asking."

The man snarled.

"There's no call to get ugly," Sloan said. "It was just a little accident."

"Who might you be?" the man demanded.

"I'm a friend of Libby's. Who are you?"

The man narrowed his eyes. "I'm Howard Bisman. I own this place, and I'll thank you to stay out of things."

Sloan gave him a cold, hard smile. "And I'll thank you to speak more kindly in front of the children."

Emily had been in the office getting a new roll of quarters for the cash register when Howard had stormed out of the kitchen. She hadn't heard the commotion in the dining room, but she'd heard the swinging door bounce off the wall, heard him bellowing about something.

Her first thought was of the girls. Howard was mad

at her and might take it out on them. She rushed from the office.

"Those kids," her boss was saying, "have been nothing but trouble since I hired their mother."

At his words, Emily froze in midstride. Then she dashed forward. "What's going on here?"

"Trouble, that's what," Howard snapped. "And it's these brats of yours, as usual."

Emily was normally the soul of politeness and calm. But nobody picked on her children. "Don't you dare call them brats. Margaret hired me, and she said they were welcome here."

"Well, my wife's not here, and I want these kids out of here before they tear the whole damn place apart."

"That's not fair," Emily said.

Sloan had to give her credit for her reasonable tone. If he opened his mouth again his words were bound to come out in a snarl.

"My girls have never caused any trouble."

"They have now," her boss growled. "I want them gone."

Janie sidled up next to her mother.

Emily put an arm around her eldest daughter. "You know I can't leave them alone at the motel."

"Tough."

Sloan had had enough. "Look, mister."

"You stay out of this."

"I won't stay out of it." In his socks, Sloan stood six feet tall. In his boots and hat, as he was now, he hit about six-five. He leaned down over the much shorter man, got right in his face and spoke quietly. "You're upsetting the ladies."

The shorter man took a step back. ''This is none of your business.''

''Oh, but you're wrong. Libby was coming to see me when she tripped over your torn carpet.''

''Libby fell?'' Emily cried.

But Sloan was on a roll and didn't answer. ''How long has that loose edge been sticking up like that? I'm surprised somebody hasn't sued you yet. Libby could have cracked her head open.''

''Libby?'' Emily craned her neck to see around the two men arguing about her and her daughter as if neither were present. ''Where is she?''

''I don't need this kind of trouble,'' Howard claimed, ignoring her question. ''Emily, you take your brats and your mouthy friend and get out of here. You're fired.''

The room was so quiet, you could have heard ice melt. Emily's gasp of shock was the only sound.

Sloan felt the pressure of steam building inside his head. Any minute it was going to shoot out of his ears. ''You can't fire her, you little weasel, she quits.''

Emily shook off her shock. ''Now wait a min—''

''Fine.'' The balding man gave a single, sharp nod that made his cheeks jiggle. ''She's fired from the motel, too. I want her cleared out of there within the hour.''

Somewhere in the back of his mind Sloan knew he was going too far, but he couldn't seem to stop himself. ''She'll be out in half that time.''

Sloan spun on his heel and reached for Libby.

The child was not there. He turned again, looking, searching.

''Where's Libby?'' Emily demanded. ''Is she all right? You said she fell.''

Sloan frowned. ''She was right here a minute ago.''

But now, he thought with alarm, she was gone.

Chapter Two

They looked everywhere. Beneath every table and chair, behind the counter, in the kitchen, even the men's room. The search took less than four minutes. Libby was nowhere to be found.

Emily felt the panic rise up and swell in her throat. Her baby was missing. But that wasn't possible. It couldn't be.

They questioned every customer, but no one remembered seeing what Libby did, where she went, once Sloan and Howard had started arguing.

''What did I tell you?'' Howard ranted. ''Trouble. Nothing but trouble.''

Outside, the roar and rattle of a semi, the *swish* of its air brakes, sent a new fear stabbing at Emily's heart. She whirled toward the door. ''The highway!'' What if Libby had decided to cross the highway? She was so tiny. Cars and trucks sped past the café at sixty miles an hour or faster. ‘‘Libby, dear God.’’

Sloan heard Emily’s desperate whisper. ‘‘Would she go out there?’’

‘‘What?’’ Distracted, horrified by visions of Libby’s tiny body splattered across the blacktop, Emily turned toward the man who had quit her job for her. A small detail about which she couldn’t be bothered just then.

‘‘The road,’’ Sloan said. ‘‘Would she try to cross it?’’

Emily swallowed. ‘‘She knows she’s not allowed to, but we’re staying at the motel over there, so she might—’’ She was rambling. It was the fear. Neither of her children had ever gone missing before. She couldn’t just stand there and wring her hands, she had to *do* something.

She made a dash for the door. ‘‘Janie, you stay here.’’

A hushed murmur spread throughout the dining room.

Sloan took command. He sent two men to the gas station across the corner, and another two to the garage west of the café. ‘‘Look everywhere,’’ he ordered them. ‘‘In every place a little girl can hide, inside and outside the buildings. Then come back here and tell Janie what you find. Okay, Janie?’’

Her face pale, eyes so big behind her glasses that they threatened to swallow her face, Janie nodded. ‘‘Okay, Mr. Sloan. But where are you going?’’

‘‘I’m going to look around out back, just to be sure.’’ If Libby’s feelings were hurt because of that jackass Bisman, there was no telling where the poor kid might have gone.

* * *

Libby's feelings were, indeed, hurt. She was crushed. But she wasn't at the motel where her mother looked. She wanted to be, wanted to curl up in the bed she shared with her sister and pull the covers over her head. But she wasn't allowed to cross the road without her mother.

Besides, she couldn't go out the front door of the café without everybody hearing the bell over the door tinkle.

She didn't want to sneak away, she wanted to have Mommy hold her and tell her everything would be all right. But Libby didn't deserve to be held in Mommy's arms. She'd been a brat—Mr. Bisman said so—and she'd gotten her mommy fired.

Libby knew what a brat was. After all, she wasn't a baby anymore, she was six. In three months she'd be six and a half. Not a baby.

But she felt like a baby as she huddled up against the back side of the big trash bin behind the café and swiped tears from her cheeks.

It was Sloan who found her as he searched behind the café.

The sound of a sniff pulled him around the Dumpster, and there she sat, huddled in on herself, arms around her raised knees, head buried, shoulders heaving with each sob.

"Ah, sweetheart." He knelt beside her, his heart breaking. "Don't let that blowhard upset you."

She sniffed and looked up at him through lashes clumped with tears. Her cheeks were soaked. "What's a bo-hard?"

Unmindful of whatever substances might have missed the Dumpster and landed on the ground behind it, Sloan sat beside Libby and chuckled. ''Blowhard. Well, it's someone who talks just to hear himself run off at the mouth. Like a big gust of wind. Lots of noise, but in the end it's nothing important.''

Libby sniffed again. ''I got Mommy fired. We're gonna be homeless now.''

Sloan slipped an arm around the child and hugged her to his side. ''Ah, sweetheart, you're not going to be homeless.''

She looked up at him like a puppy begging for table scraps. ''Really?''

''Really. Now, come on. You got your mommy all worried about you, sneaking out like this. We better go find her and let her know you're all right, don't you think? She's awful worried. You might have to tell her you're sorry for scaring her so bad.''

Sniff. ''Okay, Mr. Sloan.''

After failing to find any trace of Libby at the motel, Emily rushed back across the road. She burst through the café door just as Sloan led Libby in through the rear entrance. With a glad cry, Emily flew across the dining room and swept her baby up in her arms.

She was so relieved to have her daughter back safe and sound that it was several long moments before she realized that she was being rushed from the café, one daughter on her hip, the other at her side. Shock held her silent until they were halfway across the parking lot. There she came to a halt and stared at the man her daughters called Mr. Sloan.

''What have you done?'' she managed, stunned.

''Found your missing daughter?''

''Yes.'' She closed her eyes and took a deep breath.

"And for that I will be eternally grateful. But you told him I quit my job!"

"I'm sorry." He took her by the arm and turned her again toward the road. "But you're better off not working for that creep, anyway."

"Better off?" At the edge of the parking lot she dug in her heels and pulled her arm free from his grasp. "Better off? With no job, no place to stay? I'd say you've put us out on the street, but look around! There is no street. There's only a highway, and my car is dead." She was starting to rant; fresh panic was taking over. "How am I better off?"

Libby sniffed and quieted. "I got us fired, Mommy."

"No, honey, no, you didn't get us fired." Emily shifted Libby, still on her hip. As she kissed her daughter's forehead, she shot a glare at the true culprit. "Mr. Sloan got us fired."

The sudden bane of her existence raised a palm. "I said I was sorry. I screwed up, didn't handle it well."

Emily gave him a sickly smile. "Gee, that helps, mister. Thank you." With her stomach in knots, she turned away and faced the road. What was she going to do? Where could they go? How would they get there?

If the girls weren't with her, she would turn and scream at the man who had brought this latest disaster upon them. She would cuss and kick and maybe even punch him in the nose. But her girls were with her, and she didn't want them to see their mother turn into a madwoman before their eyes.

It was just as well, because, in all honesty, she had to admit that she'd been expecting Howard to fire her for the past three days. Ever since his wife had gone to see her mother up in Denver and left him in charge. With Margaret away, fat, balding Howard, with his sweaty hands and sly eyes, liked to play. With his female employees.

None of them went along with him, as far as Emily could tell, but she had been taken completely by surprise at his unwanted advances. He had always seemed so nice to her. But, then, Margaret had always been around.

When he trapped Emily beside the cooler, her reaction had been less than polite. She hadn't meant to give him a bloody nose. Not really. She'd never hit anyone before in her life. But when he had grabbed her breast and squeezed, she had simply reacted.

Frankly, she had been surprised he hadn't fired her then and there.

Now he had; he'd merely used today's accident as an excuse. She didn't know what to do. Dear God, what *could* she do? She had enough money to get them to Fort Smith on the bus, but the route didn't come through The Corner. She had no idea where she would have to go to get on, or how to get there if she did.

"Just how bad a spot are you in?" the man named Sloan asked.

Emily glared at him. "That's none of your business."

"I beg to differ, since I guess it's partly my fault, at least according to you."

"You helped, that's for sure," she muttered.

"Look," he said, turning her to face him. "If it's a job you need, maybe I can help."

Emily turned away and started across the empty highway toward the motel. "Well, unless it's within walking distance—'' The only things within fifty miles were the café, the motel, the garage, the gas station. ''—I'll have to pass, thank you all the same.''

''What's wrong with your car?''

Emily had hoped the man would get the message and take off, but no such luck. He flanked Janie and crossed the highway with them.

''I don't know,'' she said irritably. ''Something about the oil not circulating through the engine. They say they have to take the whole engine out, but they won't start until I have the money to pay for it. Which was why I was working at the café. I was working at the motel in exchange for a room for us.''

Sloan winced at the situation Emily and her daughters found themselves in. And he had cost her the job. Both jobs.

Well, okay. If he was the cause, he would have to be the solution. ''Can you keep house?''

''I beg your pardon?'' She passed the motel office and stopped at the door to room twelve.

''You know, cook, dust, vacuum, laundry. That sort of thing. Keep house.''

She gave a small chuckle that sounded sad to his ears. ''I don't know much else, but housekeeping I do know.''

''Then come to work for me at the ranch. We'll tow your car behind us. My brother Caleb is the best mechanic in three counties, and he works cheap.''

Emily shook her head. ''What kind of irresponsible mother would I be if I took my daughters and drove off with a total stranger?''

''Mommy?'' Libby, still riding on Emily's hip, poked her mother in the shoulder.

''In a minute, sweetie.''

"I can appreciate how you must feel," the man said. "You barely know me from Adam."

"Mommy," Libby insisted. "Mommy, he's not a stranger, he's Mr. Sloan."

Janie squeezed Emily's hand. "Libby's right, Mother, he's Mr. Sloan, not a stranger."

Emily swallowed rather than let out the scream of frustration that wanted to erupt from her throat. "Yes, honey, I know."

"Look," Sloan said. "Just wait here a minute. I'll be right back." He turned and headed back toward the road.

Emily opened the door to her room and took the girls inside. She didn't have time to worry about Mr. Sloan or his housekeeping job, Lord knew where. Take her girls and ride off with a total stranger? What did he think she was, a gullible idiot? She would have to be criminally stupid to simply take his word for anything. She had to figure out what she was going to do. She couldn't stay here any longer.

In the two minutes before the man named Sloan returned and knocked on the door, Emily came up with absolutely nothing. No job, no plan, no option other than to call her cousin Brenda in Fort Smith, but that was no option. Brenda didn't have the money to lend her to get her car fixed.

The only thing Emily knew to do was find someone to take them to the nearest bus station. She had enough money to get the three of them to Fort Smith, but she would have to abandon her car. How would she get around in Fort Smith without a car? How would she ever afford a new one?

Now, here was the bane of her existence, at her door like a pesky encyclopedia salesman.

Come to think of it, since everything was on the Internet these days, she wasn't sure they even had door-to-door encyclopedia salesmen anymore.

Lord, she must be losing it to let her mind wander into such trivial territory while a crisis loomed over her head.

She was homeless. She and her daughters had just joined the ranks of those lost souls who lived on the streets, forced to beg, or worse, for money.

"What are we going to do, Mother?" Janie asked.

Emily sighed. "I'm not sure, honey. I'm going to have to think about it for a few minutes."

Libby sniffed. "Do we hafta pack our stuff now?"

Emily let Libby slide down her hip. "Not just yet."

Then came the knock on their door announcing Mr. Sloan's return. When Emily opened the door she noticed he now carried a briefcase. She eyed it with suspicion. "What's that for?"

He stepped into the room and crossed to the small nightstand where the telephone sat. "It's to show you, hopefully, that I'm a trustworthy person." From the briefcase he pulled out a notebook computer and hooked it up to the phone line. After booting up, he logged on to the Internet and went to the Web site of a ranch called the Cherokee Rose.

"Do you know how to navigate around a site?" he asked.

She didn't, but she didn't particularly want to admit such a thing.

"I do," Janie claimed. "We use the Web all the time in school. But where's your mouse?"

"You use this," he said. "It's a touch pad. You just slide your finger over it to make the pointer move. Try it."

Emily itched to try it herself, but she stood aside and let Janie do it. The girl moved through the information on the Web site with confidence.

It was interesting information.

Mr. Sloan was, according to the site, Sloan Chisholm, co-operator of the Cherokee Rose ranch in Central Oklahoma, along with his brothers Caleb and Justin. The owner of the ranch was their grandmother, Cherokee Rose Chisholm. They raised cattle and horses and did some horse training. They had a list a mile long of awards, prizes and honors for various ranching and livestock pursuits from organizations such as the American Quarter Horse Association and Oklahoma Cattlemen's Association, among others.

Emily didn't know anything about ranching or cattle or horses, but she couldn't help but be impressed by the credentials listed.

"So how about it?" he asked.

Emily slowly sat on the edge of the bed. This man, this stranger was offering her something she couldn't provide for herself and her daughters—a way out of their current predicament. A job keeping house for his family. All Emily had to do was trust him. Quite possibly with not only her life, but the lives of her daughters.

"It would be my grandmother you'd be working for."

"Your grandmother?" Some of the tightness in her chest eased.

"She does too much, works too hard. And she hates housework. She'd much rather spend her days on horseback. But she loves kids, so she'll be glad to see the girls. I don't want you to worry about that. The job includes room and board."

He was going too fast. Her head was starting to spin. She pushed herself to her feet, but when he named the salary, she sat back down, quickly.

It wasn't an outrageous salary, but it was generous. She would never make that much waiting tables or changing motel sheets.

She wiped her damp palms on the legs of her jeans. "I'd only be able to work for as long as it took to get my car fixed." She couldn't believe she was even considering his offer.

He smiled. "Who knows? Maybe you'll like us and decide to stay."

If Emily's return smile was on the nervous side, that was to be expected. "We're on our way to Fort Smith, to a good job there, at the factory where my cousin works."

He nodded as if in deep thought. "Okay, that's fine. I assume your car's at the garage across the road?"

"Yes. It's parked in the back." She wiped her palms again. "He wouldn't work on it until I had the money to pay for the repairs."

"Why don't I go see about that while you ladies get packed?"

Emily didn't remember giving him a definite answer, but within an hour she found herself in the front seat of Sloan Chisholm's four-door pickup. Her daughters, deliriously excited, were in the back seat, their belongings were in the truck bed, and her car was trailing them courtesy of a tow bar attached to the hitch on the back bumper. The Corner disappeared behind them.

Before they had pulled away from the motel, Sloan had taken her into the motel office, where Sandra,

Howard and Margaret's thirty-seven-year-old daughter, worked. He'd given Sandra his driver's license, tag and cell phone numbers and told her that if she didn't hear from Emily that evening and again the next morning, she was to call the state police and report her missing.

That went a long way toward calming Emily's nerves. Plus the fact that they were headed toward Amarillo. Once there she could always jump ship, so to speak, and take the bus.

And lose her car. Damn.

"I don't blame you."

Had she spoken aloud? Emily blinked and looked over at the man behind the wheel. "Pardon?"

"You're having second thoughts. I don't blame you. But I'm really a nice guy. You don't have to worry."

"You raise cattle, rescue damsels in distress *and* read minds?"

He laughed. "You got it." He had a nice laugh. "You ever been on a ranch?"

"When we were kids, Michael's cousin lived on a small ranch outside Pueblo."

"Michael?"

Emily smiled sadly. "My husband."

"What happened to him?"

She stared at the road before them. The dotted white line down the center of the two-lane blacktop threatened to hypnotize her. She kept her voice low so it wouldn't carry to the girls in the back seat. "He died two years ago. Leukemia."

"I'm sorry," Sloan said. "That must have been rough on all of you."

"Especially on him." Emily gasped. "My God, I can't believe I said that."

"Why not? I'd have to assume it's the truth."

Emily flopped her hands in her lap. "It just sounded so...flippant. So disrespectful."

"To me it just sounded honest."

They fell silent, letting the hum of tires on pavement, the roar of the engine and the whispers and giggles of two little girls fill the cab.

Finally Sloan spoke again. "So how did you end up working for that creep back there, anyway?"

"I didn't know he was a creep until these past few days that his wife has been away."

"The café is a long way from Pueblo," he said.

"Are you after my life story, Mr. Chisholm?"

"It's Sloan, and I'm just trying to make conversation."

"Then suppose you tell me what a rancher from Oklahoma was doing stopping in at that out-of-the-way place in New Mexico." She would much rather hear about him than spout off the details of her life.

"Well, let's see. Two days ago I stopped in for lunch on my way to return a horse to its owner."

"And today?"

"Today I was on my way home again."

Emily eyed him carefully. "And you just happened to get there in time for lunch again?"

He shrugged. "What can I say? It must have been fate."

Emily didn't know quite what to make of this man. "Why did you come back?"

"I liked the company, the service, and, much as I hate to admit it now that I've met the cook, I liked the food. I don't suppose you can make a chicken fried steak like that, can you?''

''Is cooking part of my job?''

''Yeah. Is that a problem?''

''For how many?''

''My grandmother, my two brothers and me. And you and the girls, of course.''

''You don't have any, what would you call them, cowhands?''

''Sometimes, but they bring their lunch with them. They don't live on the ranch. You didn't answer my question.''

''What was the question?''

''The chicken fry?''

Emily laughed. ''If you want your arteries hardened, I can accommodate you.''

''You,'' he said with a smile, ''are an angel.''

In the back seat Janie and Libby held hands, crossed their fingers and tried not to giggle too much. But holding back their excitement was next to impossible. They were going to Mr. Sloan's ranch! Of all the men they had surveyed at the café, Mr. Sloan was by far the best daddy candidate ever, and both girls wanted a new daddy.

Libby had been four when their daddy died. She had two memories of him. The oldest was naturally the most vague, that of a strong, warm pair of arms lifting her high in the air until she squealed with delight. It seemed so wrong to her that the laughing strong man had one day become the pale, thin stranger in that scary hospital bed, but Mommy said it was Daddy, so it must have been true.

Libby's only other memory of her father wasn't

really of him, but of her mother standing before a shiny metal, flower-covered casket next to a big hole in the ground. Mommy had been crying that day. Libby didn't like to think of it because it made her sad.

She wanted a new daddy, one who could lift her in the air and make her squeal with delight again. One who could make Janie not be so serious all the time. One who could make her mommy smile and laugh the way Janie said she used to.

They made Amarillo by late afternoon. In the back seat the girls had been nodding off for the past hour. Sloan decided it was time to stop for the night. They would get a good meal, a comfortable night's sleep, and make the Cherokee Rose by early the next afternoon. He found a clean-looking Best Western with a twenty-four-hour restaurant next door and ample room for him to park without having to unhitch the car from his bumper.

Sloan booked one room for Emily and her daughters, and another for himself. Once in his own room he immediately called home. Justin answered.

"I need a favor," Sloan said.

"Hello to you, too," Justin said. "Where are you?"

"Amarillo. I need you to do something."

"So you'll be home later tonight?"

"Uh, no. I'm staying here tonight."

"You becoming a man of leisure? Since when do you get four hours from home and stop for the night when it's not even dark yet?"

"Since I've got passengers."

"Passengers? You're bringing the mare back? What happened?"

Sloan heaved a sigh. Justin was hell to talk to on the phone. His mind was always on ten different things at once. It was easier to get his attention if you stood in front of him and got in his face.

"No," Sloan told him, "it's not the mare. She's home where she belongs, as mannerly as a charm-school graduate, thanks to Caleb's training. Now, are you paying attention?"

"Caleb's training? What was I doing, standing around with my thumb up my—"

"All right, you helped. Now would you just listen, for once?"

"Okay," Justin said with a laugh. "I'm listening."

"I met this woman."

"Hallelujah!"

"No, damn it, it's not like that. She and her girls ended up in a tight spot and I'm just helping them out."

"Ah," Justin said.

"Ah? What do you mean by that?"

"Nothing," Justin insisted a little too casually. "Nothing at all. It's just you, playing white knight and rescuing another damsel in distress. I suppose she's pretty."

"What's that got to do with anything?"

"Ha! I'm right, aren't I? She's— Wait a minute, did you say her girls?"

"Daughters. Two of them. Are you through jumping to conclusions? I need you to go to town this evening and pay Earline a visit."

"Earline? What for? She was just here."

"I want you to send her on a vacation. Her and

Jeff. A paid vacation. Two, no, three weeks. They've been wanting to take their grandkids to Disney World. Now's the time."

Nothing but the echo of silence came over the phone line for a long minute. Then, "You want me to what?"

"You heard me. I promised Emily a job, and I told her Caleb would fix her car. She was really up against it, Justin. What else could I do?"

Justin asked slowly, "Do you know what you're doing?"

"I'm just helping out a woman in need."

"I was afraid you were going to say that."

"O ye of little faith," Sloan said. "Just because I'm helping her out doesn't mean I'm going to fall for her. She's only staying long enough to get her car fixed."

Justin's only response was a low hum of doubt.

In the room next to Sloan's another phone conversation was taking place as Emily spoke first to Sandra back at the motel at The Corner to assure her that Sloan hadn't murdered them all and dumped their bodies in a ditch, then to her cousin Brenda in Fort Smith.

"I didn't have much of a choice," she told Brenda.

"So you hopped into the car with a total stranger?" Brenda shrieked. "Are you out of your mind?"

"Probably."

"There's no probably to it." Brenda's voice raised another octave. If it got much higher, glass was going to shatter. "You're not seriously going home with the man. Tell me you're not that stupid."

Emily sighed. "I thought in the morning I'd take

a cab to the bus station. I've got enough money to get us to Fort Smith, but it means leaving my car. I don't know how I'll replace it.''

''Oh, Em. I don't know what to tell you. You know I'd help if I could, but with this damn three-year drought, Tommy says we're not going to have enough of a crop to make our balloon payment on the land this fall.''

''I know, Brenda. I don't expect you to bail me out of this mess. Maybe I should take Sloan up on his job at the Cherokee Rose.''

''What's the Cherokee Rose?''

''It's his ranch in Oklahoma.''

''Hey, Tommy,'' Brenda called to her husband. ''You ever hear of a ranch in Oklahoma called the Cherokee Rose?''

There was a lot of mumbling in the background and a muffled squeaking sound as Brenda put her hand over the phone. Then Tommy came on the line.

''What's this guy's name?'' he asked.

''Sloan,'' Emily told him. ''Sloan Chisholm.''

''Sloan Chisholm of the Cherokee Rose in Oklahoma.''

''That's right.''

''You're sure?''

''Well, I saw his driver's license and his Web site, and Cherokee Rose is painted on the door of his pickup.''

''Honey,'' Tommy said, ''you couldn't be in safer hands.''

Emily's heart skipped a beat. ''What do you mean?''

''Everybody who's anybody in the horse or cattle

business in five states or more has heard of the Chisholms and the Cherokee Rose."

"Why?"

"Because they're good people. Their horses and cattle are always the best. Rose Chisholm is like a legend. There won't be any funny business going on under her roof."

"Straitlaced, is she?"

"No, I don't mean that," Tommy said. "It's just that she's a nice lady and everybody likes her, respects her, trusts her. If you ask me, you'd be better off working on the Cherokee Rose than staying in Amarillo to get your car fixed."

Emily's head reeled from all Tommy told her. She had pretty much made up her mind to abandon her car and take the bus to Fort Smith. She hadn't wanted to, but it seemed to be the more prudent of her options.

Now, accompanying Sloan to his ranch, working there, didn't seem so outrageous. Not outrageous at all, if she believed Tommy.

In the bed nearest the window, Janie lay curled against her little sister with her back to the room. She was supposed to be asleep, but her mother's voice, as she spoke on the phone, had wakened her. Now Janie squeezed her eyes shut tight and crossed her fingers.

Please, Mother, please don't take us to the bus. Please let us go with Mr. Sloan to his ranch.

Janie didn't know if she had ever wanted anything so much in her entire life as she wanted this. Except for her daddy to get well. But that hadn't happened. Her daddy had died. Nothing had been the same since. They needed a new daddy.

Not that Mother didn't take good care of them. She took great care of them. They didn't go hungry or barefoot, like poor little kids on TV. But when Mother laughed, which wasn't often, her eyes didn't mean it, not the way they used to.

Janie and Libby had surveyed every man who came into the café whom they thought might make a good daddy. Janie had learned about surveys at school, so she knew how to do it. But only one man had seemed right for them, and that was Mr. Sloan.

As her mother spoke with Cousin Brenda and Cousin Tommy, Janie squeezed her eyes even tighter and prayed as hard as she had ever prayed in her young life. *Please let us go with Mr. Sloan. Please let us go with Mr. Sloan. Please let him be our new daddy, and let him be a good one and make Mother laugh again.*

Chapter Three

Janie's wish, at least the first part of it, came true the next morning as they loaded up into Mr. Sloan's pickup and headed for Oklahoma and the Cherokee Rose. Her grin was so wide, it made her cheeks hurt, but she didn't care. Libby's was just as big.

"What are you two so happy about this morning?" Emily asked from the front seat.

The girls just giggled and said, "Nothing."

Emily faced forward again and stared at the miles of Interstate 40 ahead of them. And worried. They seemed so eager to go with Sloan. She didn't understand why. They had never taken to strangers much before.

Oh, sure, Libby didn't really know a stranger. Everyone ate out of the palm of her tiny hand. Janie was more reserved, especially during these past two years since their father died. But it worried Emily that they seemed to be so eager to be with Sloan. They would only be at his ranch for as long as it took her to earn enough to get her car fixed. She didn't want them getting too attached to the man.

She still wasn't certain she'd made the right decision in coming with him, despite Tommy's glowing recommendation. She wasn't sure if she was sitting in the front seat of this Cherokee Rose pickup because Tommy said she should, or because, despite herself, she really wanted to be here.

A sobering thought. That she might want to take off with a stranger. Her? Ordinary Emily Nelson? Having an adventure?

Who would have thought it?

"You want to let me in on it?"

At the sound of Sloan's voice Emily gave a start. "Pardon? Let you in on what?"

"On whatever is so amusing," he said. "You're smiling like you just heard a good joke."

Emily chuckled. "The joke must be on me. I was just thinking how crazy this is, the three of us hopping into your pickup and taking off with you."

"Hey, you're safe with me."

She looked over at him. "Now there's the really crazy part. I actually believe you."

They reached the turnoff to the Cherokee Rose at two o'clock that afternoon. Sloan had thought to be there by noon, but he hadn't counted on how long it took for three females to get ready in the morning. By the time they'd had breakfast at the restaurant next to the motel, then loaded everyone up, it had been after nine.

But he wasn't complaining, not when he looked at

the three females in question. Every one of them adorable.

"Is the ranch named after your grandmother?" Emily asked, nodding toward the sign ahead that arched over the gravel road.

"Other way around," he said.

"She was named after the ranch?"

"That's right. She was born here."

"Look," Janie cried from the back seat. "Are those Cherokee Roses?" She was pointing at the sign.

Sloan pulled up before the sign and stopped. "That's right," he said.

Emily hadn't paid much attention to anything other than the words on the sign. Now she looked more closely. On the left there appeared to be a clump of red rocks—actual, small rocks, not merely a picture or painting—shaped like roses. On the right, white roses were painted.

"Which ones are the Cherokee Roses?" she asked.

"All of them," Sloan replied.

Janie leaned forward as far as her shoulder strap would let her. "The rocks are roses? Are they petrified?"

"Why would rocks be scared?" Libby wanted to know.

"Not scared," Janie said. "Old. So old they turn into rocks."

"Golly. Is that true, Mr. Sloan?"

Sloan couldn't help but smile. These girls could come up with the darnedest things. "It's true that petrified can mean old enough to turn into rocks, but that's not where these rocks came from. These rocks came from tears."

Janie frowned. "How can that be?"

Sloan glanced at her in his rearview mirror. ''Did you ever hear of the Trail of Tears?''

The girls shook their heads, but Emily said, ''I have, but I don't remember much about it.''

''My grandmother can tell you all about it.'' Sloan didn't talk much about *Nunna dual Tsuny,* ''The Trail Where They Cried.'' His grandmother made her peace with that portion of the Cherokee past long ago. For the most part, so had Sloan. But his was a fragile peace. If he thought too much about the cheating and lies that sent his Cherokee ancestors walking more than a thousand miles from Georgia to what is now Oklahoma, he sometimes became swamped with anger and sadness. Not to mention irony, since half his ancestors made the walk, while the other half—the white half—essentially prodded them along every step of the way.

But he couldn't leave the girls hanging, and the flowers and the rose rocks were things he could easily speak of. ''A long time ago—''

''How long?'' Janie wanted to know.

''Hmm. Well, let's see. It was 1838, so that's about a hundred and sixty-five years ago. That's when seven clans of the Cherokee nation were forced to walk from Georgia all the way to Oklahoma.''

''Is that far?'' Libby asked.

''It's real far,'' Sloan told her. ''It took months to walk that far. It was a terrible trip.''

''It must have been horrible,'' Emily said.

''And that's putting it mildly,'' Sloan said. ''A lot of people died along the way. It's said that the mothers of the tribe were so sad over losing their children, their families, their friends, that the chiefs prayed for something to make them happy and strong enough to care for the children who still lived. From that day on, everywhere a mother's tear fell, a white rose bloomed."

Janie's eyes widened. "Truly?"

"Truly," Sloan said. "It's that white flower painted on the right end of the sign there. It's called a Cherokee Rose, and it's now the state flower of Georgia. It grows wild all along the trail the Cherokee walked."

"Golly," Libby whispered.

"But what about the rocks?" Janie asked. "You said they were Cherokee Roses."

"I sure did. When the Cherokee finally made it to the end of the journey, right here in this part of Oklahoma, God decided to honor them for their courage. Whenever a drop of blood or a tear fell from a Cherokee, it turned into a small stone in the shape of a rose. So the red rose rocks are also called Cherokee Roses."

"Golly," Libby whispered again.

Sloan smiled. He put the pickup in gear and drove under the sign.

"But wait," Emily said. "Are you sure your grandmother isn't named Cherokee Rose? Is she named for the flower, or the rock?" Her lips twitched.

Sloan chuckled. "She looks as delicate as a flower, but she's strong as a rock. But she's not named for either. As I said earlier, she's named for the ranch. She was born here."

A few moments later they pulled up before a large white house with dark green shutters. Sloan's description of his grandmother, Emily thought, had been accurate. The woman standing on the porch appeared as delicate as a rose. Until you looked into her dark brown eyes. Those eyes didn't give away much about the woman. All Emily saw there was a mild curiosity, presumably for her and her daughters, and an inner strength that was more felt than seen.

Once again Emily questioned her decision to accept Sloan's job offer. Cherokee Rose Chisholm might want help around the house, but would she want a stranger her grandson had dragged home? A stranger with two little girls who were bound to be underfoot more often than not?

Emily squared her shoulders. She would simply have to make certain that Cherokee Rose Chisholm found no cause to regret her grandson's hiring of her as their housekeeper.

By the time she had helped the girls gather their toys and stuff them into the mesh bags they used to keep from scattering everything all over the car, Sloan had climbed out of the pickup and rounded the hood to open the door for her. When he held out his hand, she paused.

"Welcome to the Cherokee Rose," he offered.

Emily summoned up a smile and what nerve she could. "Thank you." She accepted his hand and stepped down from the pickup.

It had been a long, long time since a man had opened a door for her and extended a helping hand. The only times Michael had ever done so had been when they had both been dressed up for a special night out.

Not that Michael wasn't a gentleman, because he was. But the two of them had grown up together, and he had known, always, that she was more than capable of opening her own door and getting herself in and out of a vehicle. She had made sure he'd known it, because, frankly, she didn't care for all that hovering. She'd always secretly thought that men did that sort of thing to convince women they were helpless and incompetent without some big he-man to take care of them and open all those big, heavy, complicated doors.

She refrained from rolling her eyes at the thought. Such a gesture would be rude, when Sloan was only acting the gentleman.

Once she stood safely on the gravel driveway he opened the back door of the cab for the girls and made an elaborate flourish. "Ladies, may I help you from your carriage?"

Janie frowned. "Carriage?"

Behind her Libby giggled. She gave her sister a shove. "He's playing make-believe, silly. He means the pickup."

"I know that."

"Come on," Sloan urged. "Come meet my family."

Two men had joined the woman on the porch and stood one on each side of her. These, Emily realized, must be Sloan's brothers. She would have said that they dwarfed the woman they flanked; her head barely reached their shoulders. But their sheer size did nothing to diminish Cherokee Rose Chisholm's presence. Delicate she may appear, but fragile she was not.

The four Chisholms had the same golden, coppery skin, dark brown eyes filled with intelligence, but Mrs. Chisholm's nearly black hair was laced with gray. Not as much as one might expect on someone her age. Emily had caught a glimpse of Sloan's driver's license back at The Corner and knew he was thirty-five. That meant his grandmother had to be around seventy or older. She didn't look it. The lines on her face were few, mostly around her eyes, and her bearing was that of a young woman.

Sloan ushered Janie and Libby up onto the porch. ''Grandmother, meet Janie and Libby Nelson, and their mother,'' he added, nodding for Emily to join them. ''Emily, our new housekeeper.''

''Welcome to the Cherokee Rose,'' his grandmother offered.

''Thank you, Mrs. Chisholm.'' Emily extended her hand toward the woman.

''It's Rose,'' the woman said, shaking Emily's hand. ''And these two,'' she added, indicating the two men beside her, ''are my other grandsons. Caleb, and Justin, our baby.'' Her lips quirked.

Justin gave a good-natured roll of his eyes.

Libby stepped up and tugged on his hand.

''Hi, there.'' He squatted down to her level.

''They call me the baby, too,'' she whispered loudly. ''It's okay, they don't mean they really think you're a baby, only that you're the youngest.''

''Ah.'' Justin grinned at her. ''I guess we should let them get away with it, huh?'' His whisper was no more quiet than hers. Everyone heard, everyone swallowed a chuckle.

''It makes them feel better,'' Libby told him with a big smile.

''That does it.'' Justin tweaked Libby's nose. ''I'm in love. I'm keepin' her.''

''Now, hold on,'' Sloan protested. ''I saw her first. I saw all three of them first, so mind your manners, kid.''

Libby looked up at Sloan wide-eyed. "Does that mean you're keeping us, Mr. Sloan?"

Emily ran her tongue across her teeth, wondering how Sloan was going to get himself out of this one. Libby could trap the most wary of creatures.

"Well, for a while, at least," he told Libby. "And it means that this one," he said, jabbing a thumb toward Justin, "is generally full of hot air. He likes to run off at the mouth, so don't pay a lot of attention to him. He's a great big flirt, that's what he is."

Before Justin could defend himself, Rose ushered Emily and the girls into the house. "You boys bring in the ladies' luggage, now. No sense keeping them standing out here in the heat."

It was a large house with airy rooms that looked comfortable and lived in. The living room was huge. Emily's last apartment would almost fit within its spacious walls. At the near end three recliners and a sofa were arranged around a big-screen television. At the far end, in one corner, two wing chairs faced a rock fireplace, while a small office occupied the other corner. A desk, file cabinet and worktable, complete with computer, printer and fax machine, fit neatly beneath the staircase leading to the second floor.

Area rugs over a gleaming pine floor spoke of years of loving care. The room was not messy, but not intimidatingly neat, thank God, Emily thought.

Well, not messy if no one counted the pair of dirty socks beside one of the roomy recliners. Emily bit back a smile. She was going to feel comfortable here.

Rose shook her head at the socks and *tsked.* "Those boys." But she made no move to pick up the socks. "Here's your first household rule," she said to Emily. "If a man wants his clothes washed, he has to put them in the hamper upstairs or the basket in front of the washer out on the utility porch himself. Socks left on the floor get left on the floor until someone gets tired of looking at them, or until the smell overcomes us. Then they get tossed in the trash. No warning, no second chance. Just tossed."

Emily smiled. "Sounds like a good rule to me. Do many socks get tossed in the trash?"

"Now and then," Rose said with a deadpan look. "But not lately. They may be planning to test you. Don't fall for their tricks or they'll have you waiting on them hand and foot. They're not spoiled, but they'd like to be."

"I see." Emily smiled. "In other words, typical men."

"Typical Chisholms, at least."

Rose led her past the staircase that led to the second floor and said they would get to that later. "Tomorrow is soon enough. You'll want to get settled in and freshened up."

"Oh, but I don't mind starting to work right away."

"We'll see," was all Rose said. She led Emily and the girls through a huge kitchen with a long dining table surrounded by eight chairs. Off the kitchen, through the back door, was the utility porch. The washer and dryer sat to one side, a large chest-style freezer hugged one wall, with pegs and hooks for hats and jackets and such on the other, and at the far end there was a bathroom, complete with a large shower stall. There was a closet next to the bathroom and a long row of cabinets.

"This is where we wash up when we come in from

working outdoors. That way we don't have to traipse dirt all over the house."

"That should make my job easier," Emily said.

"That was the idea when we built it, but I don't know how much easier it makes things. Here," she added pulling open a drawer, "you'll find any tools you might need, although I doubt you'll need any. And in the cabinet we keep things like lightbulbs, washers for faucets, entire faucets, light switches, that sort of thing."

"You believe in being prepared," Emily said.

Rose closed the drawer and said, "We're more than a half hour from town. Sometimes it's not convenient to drive that far to fix a leaky faucet."

Back in the kitchen, Rose ushered Emily and the girls down a short hallway to a bedroom and bath. "Here's where you'll sleep. I hope you find everything you need."

The room was just large enough to accommodate a double bed on one wall, a set of bunk beds opposite, with a chest of drawers between and a small closet across from it. Nothing fancy, but clean and neat and welcoming, with the nice surprise of a small television on top of the chest.

"Oh, yes, ma'am." Emily's smile stretched wide. "I'm sure we will. It looks perfect. Thank you."

Rose hoped that smile meant well for the next week or two, or however long her eldest grandson meant for Emily and her daughters to stay. Sloan had never brought a woman to stay in the house before—not even under the guise of housekeeper.

Housekeeper, ha! That boy...

She wondered what he was up to. According to Justin, Emily Nelson had gotten herself into some kind of trouble and, by bringing her here to work until her car was fixed, Sloan was merely helping her out. But was there more to it than that? Her Sloan had a huge heart that was as soft as whipped cream. And no racehorse on the track ever wore a thicker set of blinders than did Sloan when it came to women.

But Rose would reserve judgment on this Emily Nelson. It was possible that the young woman was as sweet and sincere as she appeared to be. It would be a first for Sloan, to find a woman like that, even by accident. But it was possible.

And if Emily wasn't what she seemed...well, Rose would hold her judgment and see what there was to see. Maybe the wariness she felt was uncalled for. Maybe this was the woman meant to ease her eldest grandson's lonely heart.

Time, and a discreet eye, would tell.

It didn't take long for Emily and the girls to settle into their new room after Sloan and his brothers brought their luggage. Afterward, Sloan took them on a tour of the area around the house. There was so much to see, the girls were wide-eyed and practically dancing with excitement.

The backyard was small and fenced, with a pair of oak trees near the house. Beside the yard a large fenced garden stretched out in neat rows including tomatoes, okra, squash, green beans, corn and watermelon.

"Have you ever grown vegetables?" Sloan asked her.

"For years, until Michael got sick. I miss it."

"Well, miss it no more," he said. "Grandmother will appreciate any help you can give her. Like I said, she'd rather be on horseback, and it's kinda hard to pick beans from the saddle.''

''Yes, I think it would be,'' Emily said, her tongue planted firmly in her cheek.

Sloan laughed. The more he was around Emily, the more he liked her. As long as it didn't go beyond that, everything would be fine. After all, she was on her way to Fort Smith. She was only here until she could pay for repairs to her car.

He showed her and her daughters the old wooden swing hung from a cottonwood branch down by the creek fifty yards behind the house and got a kick out of the girls' excitement.

While Sloan enjoyed the girls' excitement, Emily did not. She eyed the steep banks of the creek, the five-foot drop to six inches of rock-strewn water, and firmed her mouth.

''You're not to come down here without me,'' she told her daughters.

''But, Mother,'' Janie protested. ''Why not?''

Sloan raised his eyebrows but refrained from speaking.

Smart man, Emily thought. ''Because it's dangerous,'' she said to Janie. ''You don't come here without me. Either of you. Do you understand?''

''Can we play now?'' Libby asked, looking longingly at the old swing.

''Maybe later this evening. But first we have to see what else Mr. Sloan has to show us, okay?''

''Will you show us the kittens?'' Libby asked Sloan.

''Sure.'' He pointed up in the cottonwood. ''There's two of them right there.''

Libby and Janie looked up and gasped. Two gangly, half-grown kittens, one calico, one tabby, peered down from their shared branch ten feet in the air.

"Oh," the girls said in unison.

Libby jumped up and down and pointed. "Look at them! Look, Mommy, kitties!"

"Will they come down?" Janie craned her neck to watch the cats. "Here kitty, kitty."

Her daughters' excitement nearly broke Emily's heart. She so wanted them to have pets, but since Michael's death they'd been living in a small apartment, and she hadn't thought it fair to a dog or cat to keep it cooped up indoors all the time, and she simply hadn't had the heart or energy to care for even so much as a goldfish.

When they got settled in Fort Smith, she vowed, each of her daughters would have a pet.

"They're a little skittish," Sloan said in answer to Janie's question. "They're not really pets, they're working cats."

Libby scrunched up her face. "Huh?"

"What kind of work can kittens do?" Janie asked.

"They catch mice. That's their job. Out here in the country like we are, we'd be overrun with mice and rats if it wasn't for the cats."

Emily was grateful that he didn't give the girls too much time to think about the subject of mice and rats before he led them away from the kittens, the tree with its swing, and the creek that made Emily nervous.

"Come on," he said. "I'll show you the barn, where they live."

On the way to the barn they passed a chicken house and three tool-and-equipment sheds. One shed, about the size of a two-car garage, had its double doors wide open. Her car sat inside, its grill facing out.

''Caleb will take a good look at it this evening after supper,'' Sloan told her.

''Oh. I didn't expect such quick service.''

''It won't be that quick,'' he warned. ''He'll only be able to work on it in the evenings.''

''You won't hear me complain,'' Emily said.

They turned away from the shed and headed for the huge barn, which appeared to be the center of things, with all the other buildings, including the house, spread out in a semicircle around it. Corrals angled out from either side. A handful of horses milled around in one, a half-dozen cows in the other. Janie and Libby stared wide-eyed at the huge animals. They were city girls and had never been up close and personal with anything larger than a big dog.

''Wow,'' Janie whispered as they stopped at the fence holding the horses. ''They're so pretty.''

''They're so big,'' Libby said.

Sloan chuckled. ''They sure are. You see this fence?'' He propped one boot on the bottom rail of the corral fence.

''Yes, sir,'' the girls said in unison.

''This fence works two ways. It keeps the horses in, and it keeps people out. You two have to promise me that you won't even put your hand through the fence, not to mention any other part of your body.''

''He means we can't go in there,'' Janie said to Libby.

Libby made a face at her sister. ''I know that.''

''That's exactly what I mean. You can't even climb onto the fence to get a closer look. Janie's right, those are some of the prettiest horses you'll ever see. But Libby's right, too. They're big. They could hurt you real, real bad without even meaning to. So you have to promise."

"Yes, sir," they said again.

"The same goes for the cattle in the other corral, only they're not nearly as polite as the horses. They're not pets, just big, ornery animals. You want to stay away from them, too. In fact, I want your word that you won't climb the fences or go into the corrals even if they're empty."

"How come?"

Leave it to Libby, Emily thought. She would stay away from the animals because Sloan told her to; she was a good girl. But exploring an empty corral would seem like a perfectly logical thing to do in her adventurous little mind.

"Because he said so," Emily told her.

"Oh."

Sloan chuckled. "Actually, I have a good reason for saying so. You see those doors in the side of the barn?" He pointed to the row of openings that allowed the animals to come and go between the barn and the corral. "The corral might look empty, but if there are horses inside the barn where you can't see them, they could come out and surprise you. It would surprise them, too, and you could get hurt before you could get back on the outside of the fence. So I'll take your word, all right?"

"Yes, sir," Libby said with as much enthusiasm as she might have if he'd told her she had to scrub the floor with the tip of her nose.

"Janie?" Emily prodded.

"Yes, sir," she said. "I promise. We won't go in the corrals, not ever, unless you say we can."

"Good enough."

Rose had said that the next day would be soon enough for Emily to start her duties, but Emily could not stand back and do nothing while the older woman put a meal on the table. She sent the girls to their room to watch television and pitched in to help in the kitchen.

"There's no need to make them stay in their room," Rose said. "They would probably much rather watch the big screen in the living room."

"Oh, no," Emily protested. "That's for your family. They're fine in the bedroom."

"Nonsense. While they're on this ranch, they're family, too. Besides, the big-screen is hooked up to the satellite dish. The little one in the bedroom isn't."

Emily had not expected such generosity from an employer. It made her feel a little less of an outsider, and she appreciated it. The girls would get a real kick out of watching a big screen TV, and they would be more likely to find something appropriate to watch on satellite than regular television, particularly at this time of evening. "Thank you," she said to Rose.

The girls took the news with excitement. Even steady, sober Janie grew animated when their favorite cartoon characters appeared before them in huge, brilliant color.

While the two girls stared in awe at the big screen, Emily followed Rose back to the kitchen.

The two women made a good team as they put together a huge pan of lasagna and got it in the oven. While it baked Rose pulled a bowl of green beans, which she said she had snapped earlier in the day, from the refrigerator. Emily took out the ingredients for a tossed salad.

"Oh, these are beautiful." She palmed two large, ruby-red tomatoes. "Are they from your garden?"

"Yes."

"And the green beans?"

"They're ours. We've had a good year. Do you garden?"

"I used to. I miss it. I hope you won't turn down my help out there."

"Ha! You do as much out there as you want to and I won't shed a tear. There's a small garden shed behind the house. You'll find everything you need there."

Emily smiled. "Maybe after dinner I'll go take a look, in the shed and the garden."

Rose turned on the water at the sink and washed her hands. "If you're half as eager to do housework as you are to garden, I'm going to like having you around."

"Oh, I love to take care of a home. You tell me what you want done, and I'll do it. If something's not the way you like it, just say so and I'll do my best to fix it."

"Fair enough," Rose said. "We'll go over everything after we get the boys fed up."

As if on cue, the outside door to the utility porch banged open and heavy boot steps thudded on the porch floor. A moment later the kitchen door swung open.

Emily turned and saw all three Chisholm brothers peering in from the porch. She had a smile for each of them, but her gaze lingered on Sloan. Perhaps because his seemed to linger on her.

''Wash up,'' Rose told them. ''Supper will be on the table in ten minutes.''

Sloan was used to seeing his grandmother in the kitchen at the end of the day. If he came in early enough, Earline would be there, too. Seeing two women doing the dance required to put food on the table shouldn't surprise him.

But Earline was sixty-one and, Lord love her, looked like she'd been rode hard and put up wet a few times too many. She'd had a hard life, and it showed in the deep lines on her face.

Sloan was not used to stepping into his own kitchen and seeing a lovely young woman with a million-watt smile just for him, and eyes as blue as a clear summer sky. Kinda did something to a guy's chest. Made it tight and loose at the same time. Made it swell.

''Hi.'' Which was about all he could manage out of the confusion of pleasure in his brain.

But her smile widened. Just for him. ''Hi.''

''Well, if this isn't a sight for sore eyes.'' A grinning Justin slapped his hat against his knee and maneuvered himself in front of Sloan. ''Two beautiful women, waiting just for us.''

''Don't be fooled by him,'' Rose warned Emily. ''If you'll notice, he's looking at the oven, wondering what's in there.''

Justin placed a hand over his heart. ''You wound me, Grandmother. Besides,'' he added with a wink. ''I know what's in there. It's lasagna. I can smell it. Oh, boy, I can't wait. I'm starved.''

''Wash,'' Rose ordered.

''Yes, ma'am.'' Justin gave his grandmother a wink and turned away toward the porch bathroom.

''And take off those boots,'' Rose added.

The door to the kitchen swung nearly shut. Boot steps clomped around on the porch, shuffled, then were replaced by the softer thud of stockinged feet.

As Sloan took his turn at the bootjack on the porch, he hoped his brothers weren't experiencing the same fantasies that whirled through his mind. If they were, he just might have to kill them. He should probably kick his own butt for the images he was seeing, but it wasn't as if he was *deliberately* imagining Emily greeting him in the kitchen wearing nothing more than an apron and a smile. The pictures more or less just popped into his head all on their own. What was a man to do?

Then again, he supposed if he swept her up in his arms and carried her to bed, which was what he was seeing himself do in his fantasy, she might just use that butcher knife on him.

He couldn't say he would blame her. They hadn't done more than shake hands—in fact, they hadn't even had that much contact. And here he was imagining her giving herself willingly to him in the heat of passion.

Passion that was all in his mind.

Idiot.

An entirely different fantasy teased his mind a few minutes later, after he'd had his turn at the sink to wash up. When he crossed the kitchen and stepped into the living room, he was greeted by two blond-headed angels whose faces lit at the sight of him.

"Hi, Mr. Sloan!"

It struck him that a man would willingly die—or kill—to have his children look at him like that.

But they weren't his children, these two beautiful

babies. And the woman in the kitchen wasn't his, either.

Hell, she wasn't even wearing an apron. Just jeans and a knit top. If he had any sense, he'd be ashamed of himself for that sudden burst of lust that had hit him in the kitchen. She was a woman in a tough spot; he'd brought her here to help her out, not put the make on her.

Besides, he had a family. He had his brothers and his grandmother, he had this ranch. That was more than enough for any man. He was blessed.

If from time to time he wondered what it might be like to have a family of his own making, with a woman to stand beside him, children to raise and love, well, such a dream was normal, wasn't it? And maybe someday it would be his.

But not this woman, not these children. They weren't his. They were temporary, just on their way to the better life they had planned in Fort Smith.

"Did you come to watch TV with us?" Libby asked.

Time to change gears, Sloan told himself. He gave the girls a big smile, because they made him feel like smiling, despite the sudden hollow feeling in his gut.

"I came to tell you supper's almost ready. Are your hands clean?"

Chapter Four

The next morning Emily started her new job in earnest. At exactly 6:30 a.m., the precise moment that all four Chisholms made their way to the kitchen, she put breakfast on the table. Scrambled eggs, a pile of sausage patties, hash browned potatoes, a giant stack of pancakes, a pitcher of orange juice, another of milk and a gallon of coffee.

Rose smiled. ''I could get used to this.''

''Where are the girls?'' Justin asked.

''Asleep,'' Emily said. ''It's too early for them. I'll fix them something later when they get up.''

The way everyone dug in to the food did Emily's heart good. It had been a long time since she had cooked for anyone but herself and the girls. She liked seeing the fruits of her labor being so thoroughly enjoyed.

She did wonder, though, if something was wrong.

Sloan seemed to be deliberately avoiding meeting her gaze.

Maybe he simply wasn't a morning person. He didn't seem to have much to say to anyone.

''Great breakfast,'' Justin complimented.

''Thank you. Was it enough for everyone?'' She couldn't help but ask, since every bite and crumb and sip had disappeared in short order. ''Do I need to make more tomorrow?''

''If you make more than this tomorrow,'' Caleb, the quiet one, told her, ''we'll have to widen the doors just to get in and out of the house.''

''He doesn't mean you should fix less,'' Justin said hurriedly.

Sloan scooted his chair back from the table and cast her a quick glance, the first of the day. ''This was just right.''

''You're sure?'' she asked. ''I can take criticism, you know. But if I don't know I'm doing something wrong, I can't know what to change.''

Sloan looked surprised. ''You haven't done anything wrong. Like I said, this was just right.''

''Okay,'' she said, still not certain. If there was nothing wrong with the breakfast she served, then why was he acting so strangely?

But then, she barely knew the man, she reminded herself. Maybe this silent, taciturn man was the real Sloan Chisholm. Or maybe he simply wasn't a morning person, although he'd been cheerful enough the day before when they'd left Amarillo in his pickup.

She reminded herself that her job was not to discern this man's moods, but to care for his home. She didn't need his smiles and encouragement for that. Her instructions came from his grandmother. And Rose seemed more than satisfied with breakfast.

"Well, then," Emily said as Rose and the men headed for the back door, "I'll see you all at noon for lunch."

Justin gave her a wink and put on his cowboy hat. "We won't be late."

The rest of Emily's day seemed to fly by at breakneck speed. After getting the girls up and fed, she decided to start upstairs first. There were four bedrooms, three baths. They didn't need as much attention as she thought they might. Someone had been keeping up with the cleaning. Still, there was more than enough for her to do.

The upstairs rooms spoke a great deal about the individuals who lived and slept in them. Rose's room was lovely, with bold colors and lacy runners on the dresser and chest. Everything was as neat as a pin. Her bathroom was equally neat.

It appeared that Caleb and Justin shared the hall bath. It also appeared that someone tried to keep it neat and clean, but the other user wasn't so particular. The tale was told in the bedrooms: Caleb's was painfully neat, with nothing out of place. Justin's, on the other hand, looked as if a tornado had swept through.

It was Sloan's room that drew her attention, however. He had his own bathroom; it, along with his bedroom, fell somewhere in between Caleb's neatness and Justin's sloppiness. Sloan was not sloppy, not at all. But he was not uncomfortable leaving his razor and shaving cream beside the sink, or his towel hanging crookedly over the shower rod. An extra pair of boots and a pair of athletic shoes sat outside the closet, and three empty hangers lay on the dresser. All in all, not bad for a man, she thought. Neat, but lived-in.

She spent the morning changing sheets, gathering damp towels, scrubbing bathrooms, dusting, vacuuming. She lost count of the number of times she ran downstairs to change loads of laundry. And through it all, the girls "helped" her.

They helped her later that morning, too, when she put together a meatloaf for lunch. It only took her nearly twice as long to let them help her as it would have to do it herself, but to Emily, the time spent with them was worth any amount of extra work.

As with supper the night before, the girls were thrilled to join the family around the big table for lunch.

Sloan seemed genuinely glad to have them there. And he seemed more like the nice, fun man she had met in New Mexico. It was only after lunch, as he and his brothers and grandmother were leaving the house again, that Emily realized he hadn't said a single word to her.

"What's with you?" Justin asked.

Sloan would have ignored his youngest brother, but Justin, being Justin, got right in his face the minute they were in the barn, out of sight of the house. And his tone and his smile were just a little too casual to be real. Sloan knew he would regret asking, but failing to ask would get him nowhere.

"What are you talking about?"

"You know what I'm talking about."

Sloan was afraid he did.

"I'm talking about Emily. Yesterday you staked a

claim on her and her girls right there on the front porch. Last night at supper, and again today, you barely even spoke to her or looked at her. What gives?''

Sloan wished he knew. ''Nothing gives. You're imagining things. I never staked a claim, as you put it.''

''No? Fine.'' Justin grinned and settled his hat more firmly on his head. A sure sign he was getting ready to get in a good dig. ''Then you won't mind if I move in. She's awfully pretty.''

Sloan wished he knew whether Justin was serious, or merely trying to get a rise out of him. Either way, what his little brother was suggesting was unacceptable.

''No way,'' he told Justin, shaking his head.

''Of course she's pretty,'' Justin protested. ''With those big blue eyes, that slender neck, those legs that look a mile long, she's the prettiest thing we've seen around here in a long time.''

Sloan was shaking his head again before Justin finished speaking. ''You'll get no argument out of me on that score. Of course she's pretty.''

''Then what are you objecting to, big guy?''

''You, kid. What are we running here, a singles bar? She's our housekeeper, for crying out loud. You can't put the make on our housekeeper.''

''Earline's our housekeeper—''

''Keep your voice down.'' Sloan shot a look over his shoulder toward the house. Emily didn't know they had a housekeeper; she thought she was it. He wasn't going to have her finding out any different from his numbskull little brother.

''And I'm sure not wanting to put the make on

Earline,'' Justin continued. ''Emily Nelson, now, is a different story.''

''You'll show her the same respect you would Earline, or by God, I'll—''

''You'll what?'' Justin taunted.

Taunted. He was pulling Sloan's chain, and Sloan knew it. He just didn't seem to be able to stop himself from reacting like a predictable idiot.

''The day when you can tell me what to do, big guy, is long gone.'' Another taunt. This one a blatant dare. An invitation.

''Don't count on it, kid.'' They hadn't had a decent wrestling match in months. Maybe pounding on Justin for a while would take his mind off wanting to do exactly what the kid had accused him of—stake his claim on Emily. Yeah, a nice little rumble was just what he needed. He always enjoyed taking the starch out of one brother or the other. Didn't even mind much when it was him who ended up de-starched. It was the effort that counted. ''You're not too big yet for me to teach you some manners.''

''Oh ho!'' Jason crowed.

Caleb stepped into the barn and chuckled. ''Oh, goody. Can I watch?''

Sloan and Justin turned as one and spoke at the same time. ''Butt out, *yanasa.*''

Yanasa was the Cherokee word for *buffalo.* They'd been calling Caleb that since childhood, because when he decided to get stubborn, he was about as movable as that big, hairy beast.

''What am I butting out of?''

''This one,'' Justin said, sneering and jabbing a thumb toward Sloan, ''doesn't want the new housekeeper for himself—''

"Which would explain why he's been ignoring her," Caleb said.

Sloan snarled.

"But he seems to think I should keep my hands off, too," Justin complained.

"You?" Caleb hooted. "What happened to that Harding gal in town? I thought you said you were in love. Or was that in lust?"

Justin made a face. "She dumped me. I'm heart-broken. I need a distraction."

"There's a nice little section of fence out along the highway that needs repair. That ought to be enough of a distraction, even for you," Sloan said gruffly. "Emily's off-limits. To all of us. She's in a tight spot and we're helping her out, that's all. She's got enough on her plate without having to worry about one of us coming on to her."

"Ah." Justin tucked his thumbs into his front pockets and rocked back on his boot heels like some drugstore cowboy.

"Ah, what?" Sloan snapped. This entire stupid conversation was playing havoc with his good humor.

"Ah," Justin repeated. "As in, ah, I was right. You do want her for yourself."

Sloan rolled his eyes. "Anybody ever tell you you have a one-track mind?"

"Who, me?"

"That girl in town probably thought so," Caleb offered. "Bet that's why she dumped him."

"Go soak your head," Justin grumbled.

"Go fix the fence," Sloan said tersely. "Unless you'd rather wait until it falls, then spend the day chasing cattle up and down the highway."

Justin's face lit up like a kid who'd just been promised a treat. "You think they'd get out? Hot damn, that'd be fun, riding up and down the road, stopping traffic, chasing cows. A highway rodeo."

Sloan and Caleb both groaned.

"Fix the damn fence." This time, Sloan made it an order. As the oldest, and ranch manager, he got to do that now and then. Sometimes his brothers even did what he said.

An hour later Sloan was on his way to town to buy a fan belt for his grandmother's Suburban, and he was feeling guilty as hell. Not about the fan belt, but about Emily. If both his brothers noticed that he'd been ignoring her during the few, short times the family had been together in the twenty-four hours Emily had been on the Cherokee Rose, then it stood to reason that Emily had noticed his behavior, too.

In fact, he was sure she had. That would explain the puzzled look he'd seen on her face the one time she'd caught him glancing over at her.

Well, hell. He'd probably gone and hurt her feelings. A tender little thing like Emily didn't deserve that. He would have to make it up to her. Explain himself. Apologize.

But what was he supposed to give as an excuse?

"I couldn't look at you because every time I did I had these really great fantasies...."

Nope. Wouldn't do at all. She would either slap his face or lock herself in her room to get away from him.

Still, he was going to have to come up with something.

He slowed down to the speed zone at the edge of town. He had some time to think on it. He had a couple extra errands he could run while he was in town, then it was another forty-five minutes back to the ranch. Surely in that time he could figure out a way to explain himself and put her at ease.

Emily was finding tending the Chisholm house a true pleasure. It was a home to be proud of, a home for generations to be born, grow up, raise children of their own and grow old in, at ease in the knowledge that this home would stand the test of time. Love rang within these sturdy walls.

She and Michael had had a home filled with love. Oh, the fun they'd had when they were first married. The thrill as they were blessed with first one child, then another.

The heartache and devastation of Michael's illness had tested their faith, their home. In the end, they had lost their home, sold to pay for medical bills. And still Michael had died.

Now here she was, trying to make her way to Fort Smith to build a new life for herself and her daughters.

She waited for the black talons of terror to wrap themselves around her throat, the way they always did when fear of the future, doubts of her own abilities, seized her.

But the terror did not come. It was this house, she thought. There was too much love here. It wasn't for her, but still, its warmth enfolded her and kept the terror at bay.

She checked the roast in the oven, determined that the first supper she served the Chisholms would be perfect. And if Sloan still refused to look at her, she would force herself to confront him and ask for an explanation. If she was doing something to displease him, she wanted to know. She might technically be working for his grandmother, but it was Sloan who had hired her and brought her here.

The roast looked and smelled wonderful. She had found it that morning in the big chest freezer on the utility porch. She assumed the dozens of packages of beef, all wrapped in white butcher paper and labeled by hand, were from Cherokee Rose cattle. They had enough meat in there to feed an army for a month.

But they were running low on other things, so she'd begun a list. After supper she would ask Rose about doing some shopping tomorrow.

She was going to be darned busy after supper, it seemed. Clean up the kitchen, confront Sloan, talk to Rose, and, before the sun went down, in the cool of the evening—if it ever got cool in the evenings in Oklahoma—she wanted to sink her hands into that rich, red soil in the garden. She was itching to play in the dirt. The girls could help her.

By the time the roast was ready to come out of the oven, she heard someone enter the utility porch. From all the stomping, it had to be one of the men. Rose might wear cowboy boots, but she had a quiet tread. Besides, she was already upstairs taking a shower.

Emily opened the oven just as someone came in from the porch. With an oven mitt on one hand and a thick pot holder in the other, she reached into the heat for the roasting pan.

"Here, I'll get that."

And before she could blink, she was pushed aside—gently, but definitely aside. She opened her mouth to protest, but by then it was too late. Sloan had taken her mitt and pad and was lifting the hot, heavy pan from the oven.

"This thing weighs more than you do. Where do you want it?"

Wary—this man rushing to her aid with such a thoughtful gesture was the same man who hadn't spoken to her since he'd taken her and the girls on the tour yesterday afternoon—Emily motioned toward the stove top.

"There." He set the pan down and smiled at her.

Emily's heart lifted. He wasn't upset with her, at least not anymore, if he had been. He had just gone out of his way to be nice to her. No way could he think she actually required help lifting a roast from the oven.

Her return smile was wide and genuine. "Thank you."

He shrugged in an "Aw, shucks, ma'am" sort of way. "You might have burned yourself, or dropped it and splattered hot juice all over your..." His gaze trailed down past the hem of her shorts. "...legs."

Emily felt the heat of his gaze as if the hot juice from the pan had, indeed, splashed against her. But it was not an unpleasant heat. Not in the least. It was, however, shocking. She couldn't remember the last time her blood, her very skin, had heated at a mere look from a man.

Wow.

As the heat raced upward toward her face, she spun abruptly toward the sink and turned on the cold water. She thrust her wrists beneath the cold flow and hoped he couldn't hear the sudden pounding of her heart.

The rushing sound of the water did nothing to calm

her, but emphasized the speed at which her blood was racing through her veins.

From just a look? What was happening to her?

"Emily?" Concern filled his voice. "Are you all right?"

With a deep breath, she offered him what she hoped was a steady, friendly smile. "I'm fine." He would be appalled if he knew the lonely widow he'd hired to keep house for his grandmother had a sudden case of the hots for him.

"You sure?" He took a step toward her. "You look a little flushed."

Naturally, her cheeks heated even more. She could only imagine how bright a shade of red they were. "Really. I'm fine. It must just be the heat from the oven."

At the reminder, he stepped back and blinked. The oven door still gaped wide open and three hundred-plus-degree air was filling the room. "Oh." He shut the door.

"Thank you," she said again, for lack of anything intelligent.

"Well, I'll just, uh, go upstairs and tell Grandmother her truck is fixed."

Emily turned off the water and reached for a hand towel. "She'll be pleased."

He stood there another long moment, during which Emily held her breath, hoping. That he would linger there in the kitchen? That he would smile at her again? That he would kiss her?

Before her cheeks could heat again at the thought, he finally turned and headed for the stairs.

Her hands didn't stop shaking until dinner was on

the table. Then they started trembling again, because he looked at her.

"Did you get the fence fixed?" Sloan's words were for one of his brothers, but his gaze stayed locked on her.

Justin snickered. "Was Emily going to fix the fence?"

Libby evidently thought the idea of her mother fixing a fence was funny. She giggled. Even Janie laughed.

Sloan blinked and frowned at Justin. "Emily? I was talking to you, numbskull."

This set the girls off again.

Emily frowned. "No name-calling at the table, please."

The instant the words were out of her mouth, she wanted them back. Her hand flew to her lips. "I'm sorry." She was an employee here, nothing more. What right did she have spouting rules? "You all make me feel so at home, I forget, sometimes, that... Well, you know what I mean. I didn't mean to overstep."

"Nonsense," Rose said, smiling. "You're absolutely right. There should be no name-calling at the table. Or anywhere else, for that matter. Especially around the girls. Maybe the three of you will have a civilizing influence on my grandsons."

"Civilizing?" In mock outrage, Justin placed his hand over his heart. "We're the most civilized grandsons you've got."

"A bunch of wild Indians is more like it," Rose said, one corner of her mouth twitching.

Libby and Janie covered their mouths and giggled even harder.

"Tsk, tsk, Grandmother." Sloan's lips twitched. "No name-calling."

There was no chance now that the girls would stop laughing anytime soon. Emily couldn't help but join in this time.

"Besides," Caleb added, "you know good and well that the Cherokee were civilized long before the white man ever came to this country. After all, we're not one of the Five Civilized Tribes for nothing."

Rose rolled her eyes and shot a look of helplessness at Emily. "You see what an old woman has to put up with in her own home? It's a disgrace, that's what it is. Such disrespect for an elder."

"Oh, no, Miss Rose." Janie's laughter disappeared and she spoke earnestly. "They don't disrespect you, they only tease you because they love you so much. Isn't that right?" The latter she directed at the brothers.

Emily pursed her lips to keep from grinning. *Gotcha,* she thought. Now the three grown men were going to have to openly admit how much they loved their grandmother.

The Chisholm brothers took Janie's words with good grace and smiled.

"Of course that's right," Sloan told Janie. To his grandmother he said, "We only pick on you because we love you so much."

"Then perhaps," Rose said, "I should wish you didn't love me quite so much. Please pass the potatoes."

"I forgot to ask," Sloan said. "Anybody hear from Mel while I was gone to New Mexico?"

"I saw her in town," Justin said.

"Melanie Pruitt is our nearest neighbor," Rose explained to Emily. ''She's like a little sister to these boys.''

''Men, Grandmother,'' Justin said. ''I keep trying to tell you, we're men.''

Rose nodded gravely while her eyes laughed. ''I stand corrected.''

''Is she still dating that guy from Oklahoma City?'' Caleb asked.

''Who,'' Justin said. ''Grandmother?''

Caleb smirked. ''Melanie.''

''Oh.'' Justin shrugged. ''She didn't say.''

A loud clap of thunder punctuated Justin's statement.

Emily had been unaware that outside the windows the sky had rapidly turned dark during the past few minutes. ''It's going to rain?''

''It's going to come a toad-strangler,'' Sloan told her.

''A toad-strangler?'' Libby broke up again, with Janie following right along.

''That means it's going to rain so hard,'' Caleb said, ''that even critters who like water are likely to drown.''

''Oh, no!'' Libby lost all urge to laugh. ''Mommy, the little toads are going to drown?''

''No, honey.'' Seated next to her youngest, Emily reached over and smoothed a hand down Libby's hair. ''Caleb was just teasing. It's just an expression, isn't that right, Caleb?''

Looking chagrined, and casting glares at his brothers, who were trying unsuccessfully not to laugh at him, Caleb gave Emily, then Libby, a pained smile. ''Sorry, little one. Your mother's right, it's just an expression. I didn't mean to upset you.''

"Oh." Libby grinned. "Good." Then she sobered again. "But, Mommy, if it's gonna come a toad-strangler, does that mean we can't work in the garden?"

Emily glanced toward the window over the sink behind her. "If it rains on the garden and gets it all muddy, then we'll have to wait until tomorrow." Her own disappointment took back seat to Libby's. Libby loved to play in the dirt and had been looking forward to helping in the garden. "I'm sorry, baby."

Janie speared a piece of roast on her plate. "That's okay, Libby." Janie didn't particularly enjoy getting dirty. "We'll just watch TV instead." As far as Janie was concerned, the problem was solved.

At least, until the time came to decide what they would watch on television. Libby would want cartoons. Janie would want something educational. There would be whining, on both sides.

Emily sighed and served herself more potatoes. She sure hoped the sun came out tomorrow.

At 1 a.m. another round of thunderstorms hit the Cherokee Rose. A loud clap of thunder and brilliant flashes of lightning woke Emily. She checked on the girls, but they slept on, unaware of the noise and fury surrounding the house. Her girls, bless them, could sleep through a nuclear blast.

They must take after their father, because Emily had never had the knack for sleeping through loud noises, nor for going back to sleep easily once awakened. With a sigh of frustration, she slipped on her robe and made her way to the kitchen. A small glass of milk usually helped.

The kitchen, as was the rest of the house, was dark,

but the frequent lightning helped her make her way to the counter. She felt her way to the stove and turned on the small light in the vent hood.

"Storm wake you?"

At the sound of the low, deep drawl behind her, Emily shrieked and whirled. Her hand flew to her heart, to keep it from jumping right out of her chest.

"Sorry," Sloan said from his seat at the kitchen table.

She managed one breath, then another, but they came hard, staring as she was at the strip of bare chest teasingly revealed by his unbuttoned shirt.

"I didn't mean to scare you."

She gave a nervous laugh and moved her gaze up to his face. "Well, you did. I think you just shortened my life by a couple of years, at least. What are you doing sitting here in the dark?"

"Couldn't sleep." He raised his beer bottle and wagged it in her direction. "Want one?"

Her heart was starting to settle, as long as she didn't look at his chest again, but her throat would be dry for a week no matter what she drank. "No, thanks. I came for milk." She turned and got a glass from the cabinet beside the sink then made her way to the refrigerator. She felt the need to move, to keep busy. Unexpectedly sharing kitchen space in the night with Sloan was the most intimate act she had experienced with a man in months. Years. It left her feeling unsure, vulnerable. Itchy.

"Somehow," Sloan said with a smile evident in his voice, "milk suits you better."

"Thank you." She opened the fridge and poured herself half a glass of milk. "I think."

He chuckled. "I just meant that you seem the

sweet, wholesome type, instead of the type to swill beer in the middle of the night with some man in his kitchen.''

Sweet and wholesome. She frowned over those words, wondering if they were accurate and trying to decide how she felt about their being applied to her.

''Is something wrong?'' Sloan asked, his voice quiet against the backdrop of the storm outside.

''No.'' She pulled out the chair across from him and sat down. ''No, nothing. Why?''

''The way you were frowning just now,'' he said, ''I wondered if I've offended you.''

She gave him a small, wry smile. ''Funny, but that's the question I've been meaning to ask you.''

''You've been meaning to ask me if I've offended you?''

''If I've offended you,'' she corrected. ''If I've said or done something I shouldn't have since we got to the ranch.''

He studied the label on his beer bottle as if it held the secrets of life. Or next month's beef prices.

''If you'd rather not talk about it,'' she began.

''No,'' he said quickly. ''I'm glad you asked. In fact, I meant to bring it up myself earlier this evening.''

Emily felt her stomach sink. He had changed his mind about her working here. He was going to ask her to leave. She swallowed. Hard. ''What have I done?''

''Nothing.'' He jerked his gaze from the bottle to her. ''You haven't done anything wrong. That's what I wanted to tell you.''

She cupped her cold glass of milk between her

hands and waited for a boom of thunder to fade. "I don't understand."

He drew a figure eight on the table with the bottom of his beer bottle. "I guess you probably noticed that I haven't said much to you the past couple of days."

"You haven't said much, no. You've barely looked at me."

"I know. I'm sorry."

"May I ask why?"

He let out a loud sigh. "I thought I needed to back off and give you some room."

Emily frowned. "Give me some room?"

"You know." He shrugged. "Room. I practically dragged you here, you barely know me, and I toss you into a house with two other strange men. I wanted to give you plenty of room so you wouldn't feel threatened here."

"Threatened?" God, she was starting to sound like a parrot. "I haven't felt threatened here."

"Some women might. Might at least feel vulnerable. Anyway, I didn't want you to feel that way, so I backed off."

"You mean you quit speaking to me, quit looking at me."

He shrugged again. "That's about it. I apologize if I made you uncomfortable."

Emily laughed lightly, her tension easing. She'd been right earlier when he had taken the roast from the oven for her. He wasn't upset or angry with her.

"What's funny?" he asked.

"You, making me uncomfortable because you were trying to keep from making me uncomfortable."

"Well." He laughed, too. "When you put it that way. Can we start over?"

"I'd like that. Aside from what we just talked about, you and your family have gone out of your way to make me feel at home here, and I do. You took a chance on a stranger, a stranger with two kids. Your brothers and grandmother welcomed me and my children into your home. How could I possibly feel uncomfortable?"

"I'm glad you don't," he said softly.

The deeper, softer tone of his voice made the room, the situation, feel even more intimate. Her gaze seemed to move all on its own to the bare strip of hair-covered flesh revealed by his open shirt. When she finally realized that she was staring, she forced her gaze up along the column of his strong, tanned throat, over his chin, those sharply defined lips, his straight nose and into those dark brown eyes.

He'd been watching her. She could tell by the look in his eyes that he'd watched her stare at his chest.

"It's late." She tore her gaze away, only then noticing and remembering the glass of milk in her hands. She had yet to take a sip. In two long gulps, she downed it all and rose from the table. "The storm's moved on." At least the one outside, if not the one suddenly brewing within her.

The maelstrom inside her, however, had nothing to do with the weather. It had more to do with the fact that it was the middle of the night, the kitchen was dimly lit, she was in her gown and robe with a man who was half dressed. It had to do with the way her blood rushed through her veins, hot and fast, with the way her nipples tightened, her breath caught.

It had, she thought, stunned, to do with sex.

Good grief. She hadn't even thought about sex, not in relation to herself, in a long, long time. Now here she was getting hot and bothered by a man who was merely being nice to her by hiring her to keep house for his grandmother while he saw to her car repairs.

Get a grip, Emily, she told herself silently.

At the sink she rinsed out her glass and set it on the counter. She hadn't yet emptied the clean supper dishes from the dishwasher.

Her hands were shaking. She gripped them together to hide that fact from the man behind her.

Beyond the window above the sink, rain still fell, but it was a slow, quiet, soaking rain, good for the grass and garden. She turned away, toward Sloan, doing her best to avoid looking at his chest again. She wasn't sure her pulse could take much more.

"Well." Her voice came out too loud in the quiet room. Then, next to her, the refrigerator cycled on and made her jump. "Time for me to go back to bed."

As she rushed past him toward the hall, he called her name. "Emily?"

She paused, her back to him. "Yes?"

"I'm glad you came."

She smiled at the dark hall before her. "Thanks. So am I."

Sloan listened to the soft whish of her bare feet as she went down the hall to her room. He took a deep swallow of beer. There wouldn't be much hope for sleep now, not for a while, at least. Not with the memory of sharing a dark kitchen with a woman in her nightgown and robe. A woman with big eyes and a dainty, vulnerable neck that made his fingers itch to trace its length.

Chapter Five

Happy to have her Suburban running again, Rose proposed a trip to town the next morning. They went over the list Emily had started and decided on the grocery store, the drug store, and, if they left lunch for the men at the house while they were gone to town, the ice-cream parlor.

The latter was a blatant bribe to pry the girls away from the television. They had gone more than two weeks without getting to watch much TV while they stayed at the café all day with their mother. Now they were trying to make up for lost time, and they adored the big screen.

Of course, they would much rather be outside playing, but this morning the grass in the backyard was sopping wet, and Emily didn't want them playing anywhere else. Not that anywhere else was any drier than the yard; the soaking rain that followed the second storm the night before had lasted until nearly sunup. Emily knew, because she had lain awake the rest of the night replaying every word, every gesture, every breath from her time in the kitchen with Sloan.

During the drive to town Emily enjoyed the countryside, as well as Rose's commentary.

"That's the Wilson place." Rose pointed to a squat brick house with a huge barn behind it. The barn was easily five times the size of the house. "Of course, we shouldn't call it that anymore."

"Why not?" Emily asked.

"Because the Wilsons sold out, oh, I guess ten years ago now."

"Ten years?" Emily chuckled. "And you still call it by its former owner's name?"

"We're a little slow to change around here. Set in our ways, I guess. Besides," Rose added. "The Stoklasa place is too hard to say. And we never thought city folks like the Wilsons would stick this long."

In the back seat, Janie cocked her head. "Mother, are we city folks?"

"I guess we are, honey."

"Does that mean we won't stick long?"

"For us, it does," Emily said. "We're only here long enough for me to earn enough money to get the car fixed, remember?"

"But we like it here." In the back seat, Libby leaned forward in her seat belt and shoulder harness and complained. "Why do we have to leave?"

Emily said a silent prayer for patience. "We talked about this when we left Pueblo. You said you understood."

"Oh." Libby sat back in her seat and hung her head. "I forgot."

"That's all right," Emily told her. "I'm glad you like it at the ranch. But you'll like it in Fort Smith, too."

"Will there be horses and kitties and cows?" Libby asked.

Emily noticed Rose's lips twitching. To Libby, Emily said, "When we visit Cousin Brenda, there will be."

Libby heaved a huge sigh. "I guess that's all right, then. If we really have to leave the Cherokee Rose, and Miss Rose and Mr. Sloan and Mr. Caleb and Mr. Justin and Abigail."

Emily frowned. "Who is Abigail?"

"She's one of the mama kitties in the barn," Libby said with sudden animation. "She's a tabby, and she's got five brand-new baby kittens. Mr. Sloan says we can go see them in a couple of days, once Abigail isn't so nervous about her new babies."

"That was nice of him," Emily said. "Do I get to go, too?"

"Aw, Mommy." Libby snickered. "You're a grown-up. You get to do whatever you want."

Emily and Rose shared a smile of irony.

If only that were true, Emily thought.

When they reached the small town of Rose Rock, they went to the drug store first. It would have taken them only a few minutes to make their purchases and check out, except Rose knew everyone, and everyone knew her. Neighbors—which included anyone who lived anywhere in the surrounding three counties, it seemed—stopped to catch up on the latest gossip, whose children and grandchildren were in town for a visit, who was gone on vacation and anything else of possible interest. Last night's thunderstorm was a big topic, especially for those whom it missed, but who badly needed the rain.

Emily wondered at Rose's introducing her by saying she was "helping out for a couple of weeks or so." Not once did she use the word housekeeper.

One woman, Sandra, proved bold enough to ask, "Helping out? Doing what?"

Emily started to answer, to set the record straight.

Rose beat her to it, saying only, "Oh, a little of this, a little of that. Whatever needs doing, and believe me, plenty needs doing. Did you get much rain at your place?"

"Not a drop, and I'll tell you, Jack is fit to be tied. We're about to dry up and blow away out at our place. If we don't get rain soon we'll have to start feeding the hay we've stored for next winter now, and have nothing left for winter." She shook her head in dismay, or perhaps it was disgust. "How's Earline, by the way?"

Nothing showed on Rose's face, but Emily felt a sudden increase in the tension in the air. "She's fine, just fine. I guess we better get along with our shopping. We promised the girls ice cream after lunch."

It wasn't until they were in the grocery store a half hour later that the reason for Rose's slight deception became clear. Or, more confused, depending on a person's outlook.

As in the drug store, it took them a lot longer to shop than it would have if everyone weren't so friendly. But finally their basket was filled and they stood in line at the checkout stand.

According to her name badge, the checker's name was Sis, and she, too, knew Rose and her grandsons.

"Did you get rain out at the Cherokee Rose yesterday evening?" Sis asked as she ran their purchases across the scanner.

"A half inch in under an hour," Rose reported. "Then a good, steady rain most of the night."

Libby sidled up to the counter. "It was a real toad-strangler."

Sis let out a boisterous laugh that made heads turn. "I'll bet it was, little one. And who might you be?"

"My name's Libby. This is my sister, Janie, and that's my mommy."

"Well, aren't you all just cuter than a bug's ear. Dang these bags." The ten-pound bag of flour failed repeatedly to trip the scanner. With an exaggerated sigh for the extra work, Sis keyed the information in manually. Without missing a beat, or seemingly drawing a breath, she smiled up at Rose. "Have you heard from Earline?"

"No, but then I didn't expect to, at least not this soon."

Sis smacked the heel of her hand against her forehead. "What am I thinking? She just left yesterday, so of course you wouldn't have heard from her. Imagine, working all day out at your house as usual, then going home that night and having those boys turn up on her doorstep, telling her she's been working too hard and it was time to take a vacation. Next thing you know, she's gone, the very next day, like she was afraid they'd change their minds." The big woman laughed again.

"And to think, that was just yesterday when she left. It was just so sweet of those boys of yours. I don't think I've ever heard of anybody sending their housekeeper and her husband and all three grandchildren to Disney World, all expenses paid. And as a complete surprise, with no warning at all. And that was smart on their part, if you ask me. Knowing Earline, she would have balked at taking off and leaving y'all with nobody to keep house for you while she's gone.''

Emily stared at the woman's mouth, watched the words form, heard them hit her ears. Housekeeper. Surprise trip. Yesterday. ''Rose?'' Sloan hadn't said anything about them already having a housekeeper. He'd said that his grandmother needed her help.

''That Sloan,'' Rose muttered under her breath.

''What was that?'' Sis asked.

Rose offered Sis a smile. ''Just talking to myself. How are we doing, there?'' She gestured toward the groceries still to be scanned. ''Don't forget to bag the cold things separately so we can put them in the ice chest. We're stopping for lunch, and ice cream,'' she added to Janie and Libby, ''before we go home.''

''Ah, a special treat for the little ones. We'll have you out of here in two shakes, don't you worry, you cute little things, you.''

Emily didn't push for Rose to explain about their housekeeper. She thought she would do better to get her answers from Sloan.

But she feared she understood. The Chisholms hadn't needed a housekeeper. Sloan had felt sorry for her. That's why he'd offered her the job.

It fit with what little she knew of him. He was a nice man, and Brenda's husband had sung his praises. Helping out a woman in need was something a man like him might do.

But to take her and two little girls into his home? That was taking charity a bit far.

Whatever his reasons, she had a sick feeling in her

stomach. He hadn't been truthful with her. What would happen now that she knew the truth?

Of course, she didn't know the truth. Not much of it, anyway. She knew only that they hadn't really needed a housekeeper. So why had he offered her the job? As near as she could tell from what Sis had said, at the same moment Sloan was offering Emily a job as housekeeper, their unsuspecting housekeeper was busy keeping their house.

What was going on?

"Come on, Mother."

Emily looked down to find Janie waiting for her with a puzzled look. "What?"

"Come on, we're going."

Looking up, Emily realized that she'd obviously been lost in her own thoughts longer than she'd realized. The groceries were checked, bagged and on their way out the door with Rose and Libby. She took Janie's hand and rushed after them.

While the stock boy loaded the groceries into the back of the SUV, following Rose's instructions about putting the cold items in the ice chest, the woman kept one wary eye on Emily.

Emily held her peace, what little she could find of it. She knew Rose expected her to ask questions, but her questions were for Sloan. If there was a fight to pick, it would be with him.

Once again that sick feeling settled in her stomach, the one that told her she might have to buy those bus tickets yet. If the bus even came through Rose Rock, Oklahoma.

Emily bit her tongue until after supper that evening. When the girls asked if they could go watch Caleb work on her car, she jumped at the chance to have them occupied elsewhere when she cornered Sloan.

"Can we, Mother?" Janie asked again.

"That sounds like fun," Emily told her. "Justin, would you mind taking them down to the garage to see the car?"

"Ladies." He bowed to the girls. "It would be my honor." With a flourish of his arm, he added, "May I escort you?"

Amid male laughter and little-girl giggles, the three followed Caleb, who had already left the house.

That left Rose and Sloan, both in the living room.

Emily hurriedly stacked the supper dishes on the counter and wiped off the table. The rest of the cleanup could wait until after she'd gotten some straight answers.

She found Rose at the desk with Sloan leaning over her.

"Sloan, may I have a word with you?"

Rose looked up at her grandson, then at Emily. "Uh-oh."

"Sure." Sloan straightened and gave his grandmother a frown. Then he looked at Emily. "What's up?"

So, Emily thought, Rose had not warned him that Emily had learned that they hadn't needed a housekeeper. That was interesting.

"I'll go upstairs," Rose offered, "so you two can talk."

"That's all right," Emily said. "I don't want to take you away from what you're doing. Sloan and I can go for a walk."

Not waiting to see if he followed, Emily headed for the back door. Outside she turned toward the creek, away from the girls down at the big garage in the opposite direction.

Sloan walked beside her. ''What did you want to talk about?''

She'd been thinking about this confrontation all afternoon, yet still she didn't know quite what she wanted to say. Finally, when they reached the swing next to the creek, she stared at the rushing water. What had been a shallow, tame trickle two days earlier was now, since last night's rain, a two-foot, swift flowing torrent. The collection of wet, muddy debris along the banks showed that the water had been another two feet higher not long ago.

''Emily?''

She turned to face the man who had hired her. ''Why am I here?''

''Pardon?''

''Why did you bring me, us, here to the ranch?''

Sloan frowned. ''What's this about? I told you, we needed help around the house—''

''Let me rephrase that before you dig yourself in any deeper. Why did you hire me to be your housekeeper when you already had Earline right here working for you?''

Surprise, then chagrin and guilt filled his face. ''Oh.''

''Yes, oh.''

''Who squealed?''

''Just about everyone in town today, but mainly it was Sis at the grocery store.''

He let out a long sigh. ''Her mouth always did outpace her brain. Look, it's no big deal.''

''No big deal? You lied to me.''

''I never lied,'' he protested. ''I told you you'd be

working for my grandmother, and you are. I told you she hated housework, and she does.''

''You got me here under false pretenses, and I'd like to know why.''

Sloan scratched his head. Hiring Emily, bringing her here to the ranch, had seemed like a good thing to do at the time, but she was starting to make him feel as if he'd done something underhanded, and he hadn't.

Well, not much, anyway.

''I only wanted to help,'' he confessed. ''You were out of options, and nobody should be left in a situation like that.''

''So you lied to me?''

''I wanted you to have a choice, stick it out on your own, or come home with me. I knew you wouldn't come here without the promise of a job.''

''So you shipped your housekeeper off?''

Ah, hell. ''I called home from Amarillo and had Justin and Caleb send her on vacation. She's been talking for months about she and her husband wanting to take their grandkids to Disney World. So, we sent them. They get a paid vacation, you get a job and a mechanic. Everybody wins.''

That was his story, and he was, by God, sticking to it. There was no sense in complicating the situation any more that it already was.

''What else?'' she demanded.

''What do you mean?''

''There's something else you're not telling me.''

''About what?''

''About why you brought me here.''

Sloan propped his hands on his hips and met her gaze. Her steady, open gaze that he could not lie to.

"Ah, hell." He stared up at the clear blue sky for a minute, then looked down at the damp ground between his boots. This shouldn't be so hard, telling a woman he liked her. Why wouldn't the words form on his tongue?

"I'm waiting," she said.

"Does anybody ever hold out on you?"

"Not for long, and don't change the subject. You were about to come clean."

He let out a long, slow breath. "All right." He walked over and turned the tire upside down and around to empty out the standing water. No sense breeding any more mosquitoes than they had to. "I wanted you to come to the ranch so I could spend more time with you."

Emily opened her mouth to say something, but he held up his hand to stop her. Which was just as well, since she had no idea what she'd been about to say.

"No," he said. "Let me get it all out while I'm on a roll. I wanted to spend more time with you because I'm attracted to you. Which was what I was trying to hide by steering clear of you, for which I apologized last night."

She stared up at him without blinking. What had he just said? "You're attracted to me?"

He clenched his teeth and nodded.

"You're attracted to me."

"Well you don't have to look so damn unhappy about it."

"No," she said, her mind whirling. "No, actually, I think I'm flattered."

He snorted in disbelief. "You look scared to death."

It was disconcerting, Emily thought, that he could

read her so well. She was scared. Confused. At a complete loss.

''Do you react this way every time a man tells you he's attracted to you?''

He'd been so kind to her, offering her this job, offering his brother to fix her car. She didn't know what she and her girls would have done without him. And now he was being honest with her. The least she could do was be honest in return.

''No. I'm sorry,'' she said. ''It's not that.''

He shifted from one foot to the other, his forehead furrowed. ''It's not what?''

''You're right, I am afraid, at least a little.''

''Because I'm attracted to you? Believe me, the last thing I wanted to do was make you afraid of me.''

She shook her head, frustrated at not being able to find the words to make him understand. ''I'm not afraid or offended that you're attracted to me. I said I was flattered, and I meant that.''

''Then what is it, Emily?''

She stared at the tire, wishing it wasn't still wet. At least swinging on it would give her something to do. ''You need to understand that Michael has been the only man in my life. I fell in love with him in first grade, and, miracle of miracles, he fell right back. From that day on there was never anyone else for either of us.''

''I see.''

''No,'' she said, ''I don't think you do. I haven't been blind all these years. Now and then I have noticed that a man looked as if he might be attracted to me. But I was so wrapped up in Michael that it really meant nothing to me. It was flattering, of course. I'm not without an ego.''

"But this time you don't have Michael to shield you from it?" Sloan asked.

"It's not that." Damn it, why couldn't she just come out and say it? She took a deep breath, and plunged. "What scares me this time is that I think it might be mutual, and I don't know what to do about it."

Sloan's pulse beat slow and hard. She had managed to surprise him. He moved two steps closer, but not close enough to pressure her. "What do you want to do about it?"

She shook her head and moved back a step. "I don't know. Nothing."

"We've just admitted we're attracted to each other and you don't want to do anything about it?"

She gave a jerky shrug that spoke of nerves. "I mean, what's the point? I'm on my way to Fort Smith. I'll only be here another week or so, just until my car's fixed and I can pay for it."

"If that's the only problem," he said, giving her a teasing grin, "I can arrange for it to take weeks, months, for your car to be fixed."

Her eyes widened in shock, then she laughed. "Shame. You had me there, for a minute. You wouldn't do that." Her expression turned wary. "Would you?"

"Naw, I guess not. But the thought has merit." His gaze lowered to her full, lush lips. What was that saying? In for a penny? He moved closer, much closer this time. "There's something I've been wondering since the first time I saw you."

Emily's heart raced. She wouldn't back away this time. Couldn't, since her feet seemed to have taken root in the damp soil beneath her shoes. Not to mention that if she moved back so much as an inch she'd be flush against the tree.

"Are you afraid of me?"

The look in his eyes mesmerized her. His deep voice washed over her and left goose bumps in its wake. "No." It was her reaction to him that was cause for concern.

"Good. Then you won't mind if I do this." He leaned forward.

His warmth surrounded her, yet he wasn't touching her. Closer, closer he came until his breath puffed against her face. He was going to kiss her. And heaven help her, she wanted him to.

He did. Just the slightest brush of his lips to hers, no pressure. Before she had time to be disappointed, he was back, a little more this time, a little longer.

Oh, he was good at this.

She refused to let herself think about this being her first kiss in more than two years. She wasn't much capable of thought anyway, since her mind went all fuzzy when Sloan whispered her name against her lips. Her mind went fuzzy, her knees went weak, and she ended up with her back against the tree and her arms around his waist. And, oh, it felt so good. She let herself sink into the kiss, into him.

Sloan felt her surrender and deepened the kiss, but not too much. He didn't want to push her too hard, too fast. Her taste was sweet and light. He dipped in with his tongue for more. When she met him with her own, he shuddered. He could get used to this, to her, the taste of her, the feel of her pressed against him. He wanted to cup her breasts in his hands, but he settled for cupping her face.

Her skin was soft and satiny, as he'd known it

would be. The shape of her, small and curved in all the right places, fit against him like a long-missing puzzle piece.

He wanted to scoop her up in his arms and carry her away to some soft, comfortable place where she would never have another worry. She wouldn't have to travel four or five states for a chance at a damn factory job just to put food on the table. Her car wouldn't quit and leave her stranded. She wouldn't be alone in life, in raising her daughters.

Realizing where his thoughts were going, and that he had deepened the kiss far more than he'd intended, he lightened the pressure and slowly broke away. He was breathing hard. His palms were damp.

The woman definitely got to him. He leaned his forehead against hers. Her eyes were closed, her breathing just as rapid as his. "I'm going to want to do that again," he warned her softly.

Her lips curved. "You are?"

"Yes, ma'am." He stood back and placed his forearms on the tops of her shoulders. "What are my chances?"

She blinked her eyes open and smiled. There was a bit of the devil in that smile. "I'll think about it and let you know."

"I reserve the right to try to persuade you."

She smiled at him, then changed the subject. "I need to go check on the girls."

"They're down at the garage. I'll walk with you."

They turned and walked away from the rushing creek and the kissing tree. After a few steps, she spoke.

"Let me make sure I've got this straight. You offered me a job, sent your housekeeper on vacation and brought me here.''

Sloan felt his cheeks sting. Damnation, he was blushing! He'd thought this discussion over. ''Guilty.''

''And spent the first two days ignoring me so I wouldn't know you were attracted to me.''

''We've been through all that.''

She folded her arms across her chest, her gaze centered on the big garage beyond the barn. ''You said you ignored me so I wouldn't feel uncomfortable. Why would your being attracted to me make me uncomfortable?''

''It did, didn't it?''

Her lips quirked. ''I obviously got over it. But you didn't know about my reservations, so what made you think that?''

Sloan stopped walking and glanced up at the sky again, but no divine intervention swept down from above to save him from this awkward, embarrassing discussion. ''I was afraid that if you knew I was attracted to you, you might think I expected you to do something about it.''

Finally, she blinked. ''Do what?''

''I don't know.'' He was yelling, he realized, but couldn't seem to help it. ''Come on to me or something, because you thought you owed it to me for helping you out.''

She pursed her lips and arched her eyebrow. ''You don't want me to come on to you?''

''Of course I want you to come on to me,'' he bellowed. ''But not just because you think you owe me something.''

''As if I would. How can you possibly be attracted

to a woman you think has no brains? No—'' She held up a hand. ''Never mind. You're a man. Enough said.''

''Hey, I resemble that statement.''

She laughed. ''Yes, you do.''

That fast, Sloan's good humor was restored. And his attraction for this woman grew. ''So,'' he said, ''you're not mad?''

She sighed and smiled. ''How can I be?'' She threw her arms out and laughed. ''When you did it all for love?''

''I knew you'd— *What?*''

The pretty woman before him, with the big blue eyes and delicately arched neck, laughed so hard she had tears streaming down her cheeks.

''Oh,'' she managed, ''you should see the look on your face.''

His knees turned to water. His mouth dried out. ''I never said anything about...about love.''

She laughed again and patted his arm. ''Relax. I think I'm actually flattered that you went to all this trouble. And that you don't expect anything more from me but an honest day's work filling in for Earline.''

''Well, of course that's all I expect.''

''And the occasional kiss?''

''The occasional kiss,'' he said quietly, ''is something I would like very, very much. But it's not part of your job description. That's what I've been trying to tell you.''

''I wish you'd told me from the start,'' she said.

''I was afraid if I tried too hard to reassure you, you'd think I was really up to something. And just out of curiosity, why did you even trust me enough to come with me? Not that I'm complaining,'' he added quickly.

She chuckled and started walking again. ''I didn't.''

''Pardon?''

''I trusted you enough to get me out of New Mexico, but when we stopped at Amarillo I decided I would either leave my car there and take the bus to Fort Smith, or I'd stay in Amarillo and get a job there until I could get the car fixed.''

Sloan stared at her and nearly tripped over a rough spot in the ground. ''For a woman with two little girls, either one of those might have been smarter than trusting a stranger.''

''Not that you're complaining.''

''Right. So why didn't you do one of those? What changed your mind?''

''Your reputation, and the reputation of your family and ranch.''

''Pardon?'' Damn, he was starting to sound like a parrot.

''I called my cousin in Fort Smith to tell her what had happened and where we were. I told her what I was thinking about doing, but when her husband heard your name he said I'd be smarter to take you up on your offer. He personally vouched for your honesty and integrity.''

Sloan's eyes widened. ''Do I know him?''

She shook her head. ''I doubt it. Tommy—Hargrave—has a small farm and ranching operation just outside Fort Smith. But he's heard of you, and he assured me that Cherokee Rose Chisholm wouldn't allow any foolishness under her roof.''

''Well, he got that right.'' Sloan relaxed and

smiled, a little humbled by such a glowing recommendation from a stranger, but gratified nonetheless. Especially since it got Emily and her girls to come to the ranch with him.

He'd have to thank this Tommy Hargrave someday.

Emily all but hummed to herself on her way to the garage. Sloan was attracted to her. If she thought about it very much, it might trouble her. After all, she'd only ever been with one man in her entire life. What did she really know about men and how to deal with the situation when a man said he was attracted to her? When a man kissed her beneath a tree?

But she didn't let herself think about it. She didn't let herself think about how out of her depth she felt, how nervous. How excited. For now, until she could be alone with her thoughts and her heart in the dark, she was simply going to enjoy the fact that the strong, handsome, kindhearted man walking beside her was attracted to her.

She heard the little-girl giggles and grown-man laughter before she had a good view into the garage because the big main door stood propped open, blocking her view.

She saw Justin first, and he spotted her. He pulled a round yellow sucker from his mouth and spun away.

"Mommy alert," he hissed.

More little-girl giggles.

By the time Emily stepped around the gaping door and peered inside the garage, Caleb, his fingers black with grease, was leaning over her engine beneath the raised hood of her car. The white stick of a sucker protruded from his mouth as he oh-so-nonchalantly looked over at her and smiled.

Too nonchalantly, she thought.

On the other side of the car stood Justin and her daughters, all three of them grinning from ear to ear, their hands behind their backs. Telltale smears of green decorated Janie's mouth, while Libby's bore purple.

Emily pursed her lips and folded her arms. ''Suckers.'' It was a long-standing joke among them. Emily always told them they couldn't have sweets, but she generally provided one after supper. ''Caught you.''

''Busted,'' Justin muttered out the side of his mouth. ''What'll she do to us?''

Both girls mashed their lips together to keep from laughing.

''Offer her a bribe,'' Caleb suggested casually, his gaze focused on the grimy engine.

''What's the deal? Who's offering a bribe to who?'' Sloan stood beside Emily.

''Whom.'' Emily's correction came automatically. She was used to correcting her daughters. But she winced, realizing Sloan might not appreciate it. She glanced at him warily.

He chuckled. ''Okay, whom, Grandmother.''

''Sorry,'' she muttered.

''Don't be. What about this bribe business?''

''Unless I miss my guess,'' she said, ''I am about to be offered a bribe because I've caught them red-handed.''

''Red-handed at what?''

Janie and Libby couldn't hold it in any longer and broke out once more in giggles.

God, but it did Emily's heart good to see Janie

giggle like a normal little girl. She was always so serious, Janie was, since Michael fell ill. She'd been so little, but she had somehow understood that her father was terribly ill. Now, just two days on this ranch, around these rough, tough cowboys, and she was giggling.

"At these," Libby told Sloan, pulling her sucker from behind her back. She waved it at him, then popped it into her mouth.

Janie and Justin did the same.

"Suckers are no-no's, huh?" Sloan asked.

"We're supposed to ask first," Libby confessed, totally unrepentant, if the grin on her lips and the twinkle in her eyes were anything to go on.

Janie leaned toward Justin and shoved her glasses into place. "Offer her the grape one."

"Think she'll go for it?" he asked.

"Yes, sir."

From his hip pocket Justin pulled a sucker wrapped in purple paper. "Care to join us?" he offered Emily.

With a laugh, Emily rounded the front end of the car and reached for the sucker.

At the last second Justin snatched it back and held it out of her reach.

"Hey!" she protested.

"If you take it, you can't lecture anybody about sweets for a whole week."

Emily narrowed her eyes. "Twenty-four hours."

"Three days," he countered.

"Twenty-four hours," she repeated, "and I won't mention this little episode at all."

Justin frowned down at the girls. "What do you think? Shall we call it a deal?"

Both girls nodded.

"Quick," Libby said, "before she changes her mind."

From where he stood near the door, Sloan took it all in with a quiet sigh. What a picture. Two little girls and a pretty woman, laughing and giggling in his garage. Who would have thought he would ever see such a beautiful sight?

Chapter Six

Melanie Pruitt pulled up and parked her pickup in front of the Chisholm home. All the way over here she'd been telling herself that this wasn't as bad an idea as it sounded. All she wanted to do was check out the woman who was ''helping out'' since the guys suddenly decided to send Earline, along with Jeff and their grandchildren, off to Florida. In the middle of summer, no less.

Melanie knew what people were going to think when word spread that she had come to meet the woman. And word would spread. Fast. People would say she was jealous, that she wasn't really over her lifelong infatuation with Sloan, despite her avowals of the past couple of years. She couldn't say she would blame them for their assumptions. She'd said she was over him a dozen times through the years.

But this time it was true. This time it had finally

sunk in: first, that Sloan was never going to be anything more than a big brother to her; and second, she honestly liked it that way.

It had never been real love that she'd felt, anyway. How could it, when it had started so many years ago?

It had been a combination of her mother's prodding—which only years later would Melanie come to understand was part of her mother's own private agenda, to see her daughter married to one of the "great and mighty Chisholms"—and Melanie's own case of hero-worship, begun the day when she was five, and Sloan, an older man of twelve, pulled her from the pond.

From the moment she told her mother about the wonderful boy who had helped her, Melanie had unknowingly—but willingly—been pushed in his direction.

"Eat your vegetables, Melanie, so you can be strong and healthy. I bet Sloan only likes strong, healthy girls."

"Let me tie this ribbon in your hair. You might see Sloan today, and you want to look pretty for him, don't you?"

Even her father had picked up the habit of using Sloan's name to get her to do things. "You let that dang calf get away, girl. You wanna get Sloan's attention, you're going to have to be a better cowgirl than that. Try it again."

It had been inevitable, she thought, that she would grow up believing that she was *supposed* to do everything in her power to attract Sloan's attention, to please him, to make him like her. It had never occurred to her to act any other way.

Sloan had, for the most part, treated her kindly, and

he did like her, but never the way she'd wanted him to. When she'd reached her teens and began to realize he might never think of her as anything other than an amusing nuisance, although, to him, a cute and lovable one, she'd needed a shoulder to cry on.

Why take it out of the family? She had turned to Caleb. Not for love, but for comfort. He'd been her friend, her confessor, her steady rock when her world began to crumble. Caleb was the salt of the earth. The best.

With her heart still set on Sloan, and with Caleb to lend an ear and a shoulder for her tears when things didn't go well, Melanie turned to Justin for pure fun. It was with Justin that she'd shared the thrill of egging the school principal's house on Halloween. The first time she'd gotten drunk had been with Justin, too. But when it came time to be sick and puke her guts out from too much beer, it was Caleb who held her head and wiped her face when the humiliating incident was over.

Oh, yes, she had something going with each of the Chisholm boys.

She still sometimes leaned on Caleb's shoulder, and when Justin wasn't involved with anyone, the two of them now and then went out and raised hell, just for the hell of it.

But Sloan? Sloan was never going to be hers. She knew that now, and she'd made her peace with it. In truth, she had come to realize that she didn't want him to be hers. Go figure. She was a fickle female.

But that didn't mean she was going to stand calmly by and watch some lazy gold digger sink her claws into him and break his heart. That's what what's-her-name, Connie Sue Walters, whom he'd fallen for a couple of years ago, had done, the worthless, silly twit. When Melanie had first met her she'd thought the woman must surely be putting on an act. Nobody was that dense, that helpless.

"Oh, Sloan," Melanie mimicked in a singsong voice, "my shoe's untied. Can you help me?"

Ugh. The really hideous thing was that Connie Sue really had been a helpless twit. What Sloan had ever seen in her was beyond Melanie.

No, she thought, that wasn't true. Sloan was a kind, softhearted man. He'd seen a damsel in distress and, like a knight on a white charger, he had ridden to her rescue and changed a flat tire for her. She had needed him, and Sloan needed to feel needed.

But when he had realized Connie Sue had needed him for every little damn thing, he'd gotten tired of it. Plus, he had realized that a woman like that would never survive long on a ranch, and Sloan's life was the Cherokee Rose. He would never leave it.

Too bad Donna Daniels hadn't known that from the start. She could have skipped over Sloan and moved on to the next sucker, saving Sloan a great deal of heartache in the process.

But nooo, Donna had to go and pull the helpless female act on him, and he'd fallen for it, hook, line and sinker, bless his little pointed head.

Men could be so dumb. Stick a big pair of boobs in front of them and they lost all sense.

She glanced down at her adequate but average chest and shrugged. She would rather a man respect her mind and heart.

Donna had had a mind, though. A tough, calculating one. She had played Sloan like a fish. Once she'd had him on her string, she'd had the nerve to mention that he should sell his share of the ranch and buy her a house in Dallas.

Melanie chuckled and killed the engine. It had probably taken a week for the dust to settle after Sloan's hasty departure from that sticky relationship.

The poor man just didn't seem to have any sense where women were concerned. And now, according to what little she'd gotten out of Justin when she ran into him in town last night, Sloan had gone and rescued another damsel in distress. And this one with two kids, no less.

Melanie considered it her "sisterly" duty to check this woman out. Maybe a few well-placed words would send the bimbo packing.

She picked up the box from the passenger's seat—after all, showing up without a legitimate excuse wouldn't do for this visit—and climbed out of the truck.

On her way to the front door she glanced around but saw no one. They must all be out in one of the pastures or someplace. She hoped she'd timed it right and the woman would be alone in the house. But even if she wasn't, Melanie could still ask a few pointed questions and form an opinion.

She decided to be polite and ring the doorbell.

When no one answered she rang again. Then it dawned on her that the noise she heard was probably the vacuum cleaner. It would be hard to hear the bell over that. She turned the knob and let herself in.

She called out, "Hello!" and pounded on the open door.

With the roar of the vacuum filling her ears, Emily worked around the pair of socks beside the recliner.

The loud voice from only a few feet behind her startled her. She whirled toward the door.

A woman stood there, dark, shoulder-length hair pulled back and tied at her nape, a clear, flawless complexion and bright green eyes.

"Hello?" Emily said.

"Hi." The woman, about Emily's own age, smiled. "I'm sorry to startle you. I'm Melanie Pruitt from next door."

"Oh, yes." Emily remembered hearing the family speak of her. "The nearest neighbor." She released the vacuum and extended a hand. "I've heard the family speak of you. It's nice to meet you. I'm Emily."

Melanie met her offer with a strong handshake.

But when Emily had released the vacuum—without, she would soon regret, turning it off—she must have jerked it or given it a small nudge. It suddenly made a horrible grinding noise.

"Oh, my word," she said with disgust. She had sucked up a sock. She shut the unit off immediately. The silence, except for the sound of the washer out on the utility porch, was blessed. "Excuse me a minute, will you?"

She turned the vacuum on its side so she could get to the rollers on the bottom, and there was half the sock sticking out. She gave it a tug, then another, harder one. The rollers grudgingly turned backward and disgorged the sock.

She grabbed its mate from beside the recliner and carried them both to the kitchen trash.

"That'll learn him," Melanie said.

Emily pursed her lips. "If only," she muttered to herself. Then, "I'm sorry, but the family is all out somewhere on the ranch right now. Is there anything I can do for you?''

''Oh, no, I just came over to drop off these.'' She raised the box she held, but before she could say anything else, or Emily could see inside or ask what was in it the back door crashed open.

''Mommy, mommy,'' Libby wailed. ''Mommy, I hurt myself!''

''Libby?'' Emily took off at a dashing run toward her baby. ''What happened? Where are you hurt?''

Libby wailed again, giant tears streaming down her cheeks. ''Here.'' She bent her arm up and pointed at her elbow. ''I falled down.''

''You fell down,'' Emily corrected automatically. Libby knew the right word to use, but when she got upset she sometimes lapsed into baby talk.

''I told her it wasn't that big a deal,'' Janie said with the disdain of one of advanced years. ''It's just a skinned elbow.''

''Yes,'' Emily said. ''But I bet it hurts, doesn't it, baby.''

Libby sniffed. ''Uh-huh.''

It was barely a scratch, but Libby liked to milk life's little injuries for all they were worth. This small scrape should be worth at least a little cooing, a bandage she could show off and a kiss or two.

''Poor baby.''

''Who's that?'' Libby asked, pointing at Melanie, already forgetting her injury.

''I'm Melanie.'' Melanie placed her box on the kitchen counter and came to inspect Libby's elbow. ''Looks like you got a pretty good boo-boo.''

''That's not a real boo-boo,'' Janie said from where

she leaned against the open back door. ''It's barely even an owie.''

Janie, Emily thought with gratitude, had certainly come out of her shell since they'd arrived at the Cherokee Rose.

''Melanie,'' Emily said, ''these are my daughters, Libby of the great and terrible wound, and Janie-the-Elder. Say hi to Miss Melanie, girls.''

''Hello, Miss Melanie,'' they said in unison.

''Hello to you, too,'' Melanie responded.

''Excuse us a minute, will you, Melanie, while I take Libby to the bathroom and clean this up? Janie, come inside and close the door.''

Janie started to comply, then stopped and shrieked. ''Mother! Water! It's spraying everywhere!''

''Water? Sit here in this chair, Libby, while I see about this. Excuse me,'' she added to Melanie.

At the door to the porch Emily stopped short. ''Oh, my word.'' A geyser of water shot from behind the washer, where the hose from the washer connected to the faucet in the wall. It sprayed clear up to the ceiling, showering a good half of the porch. Washer, dryer, freezer. Walls, floor, ceiling. Sopping.

Melanie took a look at the mess. ''Yikes.''

''Yeah.'' Emily sighed. ''Well, fixing it probably won't take nearly as long as cleaning up the mess.''

''Fixing it?''

''It won't take long.'' Water splayed beneath each footstep as Emily stepped up to the washer. First she slapped the knob to shut off the machine, then she reached over to the wall and turned off the water at the faucet. At least it was the cold that was spraying. She wouldn't have to worry about getting scalded.

Which was a good thing, since she was already drenched.

"Mommy's all wet." Libby giggled, forgetting her terrible injury.

The problem causing the leak was easy enough to spot—the thick rubber hose had split at the fitting on the end. She didn't suppose the Chisholms kept a spare hose lying around in some handy, obvious location. She couldn't be that lucky.

But she was that lucky. The gods of plumbing smiled on her when she opened the cabinet beneath the tool drawer. Right there in plain sight lay a package of replacement hoses for a washing machine.

"I must be living right." Finally. Finally something in her life went right. *Thank you, Lord.*

Emily wasn't a tool purist. If a good pair of pliers would do the job, she would take them any day over some fancy specialized wrench. She took the pliers from the tool drawer, the package of replacement hoses from the cabinet and set them on the dryer. Then she unhooked the split hose from the faucet.

Now came the fun part. She had to pull the washer out from the wall; the hose connection was on the back of the machine, down near the floor. Impossible to reach without moving the machine away from the wall. But since it sat flush between the dryer on one side and the wall on the other, it had to come all the way out.

It had to come out, regardless, so she could mop up the water and dry the floor. But if she didn't take care of some of this water on the floor in front of the washer first, she was likely to slip and end up on her rear.

When the floor before the washer was dry enough

to suit her, she opened the lid of the machine, grabbed where she could and tugged. It barely moved. She repeated her efforts, grunting this time with exertion. It moved a little farther, but not much.

"Need some help?" Melanie offered.

"I think I do, if you can find a place to grab on."

Together they managed to pull the washer far enough away from the wall for Emily to crawl behind it and replace the hose. The hose, which, of course, still had water in it, but what the heck, she thought. It was still wet behind the washer anyway.

She took care of both the hose replacement and the rest of the water in short order, and Melanie helped her push the washer back into place.

Then, to be safe, they pulled out the dryer so Emily could mop and dry the floor beneath it.

The entire event took approximately ten minutes.

"You know," Melanie said thoughtfully, "something isn't right, here."

Emily straightened from giving the floor in front of the door a final wipe with a towel and turned. "What do you mean?"

"Well." Melanie narrowed her eyes and tapped the tip of her index finger against her lower lip. "It's true that I've never replaced a washer hose myself, but I've seen men do plumbing repairs like this and something's missing."

Emily frowned. "The hose is replaced, the floor is dry and clean and the machines are back where they belong." She reached over and turned on the water and started the washer again. It sounded perfect. "What could be missing?"

"First, you didn't use any swearwords."

"Not out loud, anyway. Little ears, you know."

"Hmm. Yes. But another thing, your knuckles aren't bleeding, there are no new holes in the wall, you had the part you needed and you knew where it was."

Emily grinned. "I confess, all that's true."

"But the main thing you did wrong as far as I can see is that you didn't have to have three buddies over for a six-pack of beer in the middle of the project, while the wet laundry sat in the tub and soured."

Emily burst out laughing. "I won't tell if you won't."

"Mommy," Libby called from the table, "what about my owie?"

"I'm coming, baby. Excuse me, Melanie, I'll just be a minute."

Melanie chuckled and stepped aside. "No problem. Take your time."

It didn't take any time at all to carry poor, wounded Libby to the bathroom and tend to her scrape, and they were back in the kitchen with Janie and Melanie.

Emily walked over to Melanie and stuck out her hand. "Hi. I'm Emily Nelson. You must be Melanie from next door. What can I do for you?"

Melanie burst out laughing. "Oh, I think I'm going to like you, Emily Nelson. I think we should celebrate the new washer hose, and young Libby certainly deserves a reward for her owie. And Janie for sounding the alarm on the washing machine."

"A celebration it is, then," Emily agreed. "I don't think a small dip of ice cream will do too much harm." She smoothed a hand over each daughter's hair. "They'll still eat like little piggies at supper tonight."

Libby scrunched up her nose and snorted like the little piggy she'd just been named.

"Not only ice cream," Melanie declared. "Our blackberries are going crazy this year. I brought a couple of pies."

"Oh, but you brought those for the family," Emily objected.

"Trust me," Melanie said, lifting her pies from the box she'd placed on the counter. "If you're living in their home, they think of you as family. Besides, I baked them, so I get to say who eats them."

"Well, then." Emily took plates down from the cabinet.

"We'll have pie," Melanie said.

"And ice cream," Emily added.

"And ice cream. And you can tell me how you met Sloan and ended up out here in the middle of Oklahoma."

Sloan had wanted to come in that evening before everyone else. He'd planned it that way. He wanted, if possible, a few minutes alone with Emily.

It wasn't the first time in his life that he'd been hot after a woman, but this felt somehow different. He could recall plainly the feeling of looking forward to the next time he would see a particular woman. Pleasant anticipation, sometimes strong, sometimes merely…pleasant.

Today's feeling was different. More intense. He hadn't thought, *It'll sure be nice when I get to see her again.* No, he'd felt as if he *had* to see her again, and soon.

Of course he'd known all day that she would be

waiting at the house when he returned. He only wished he knew she was waiting for him, specifically.

But coming in early meant leaving both his brothers, their two hired hands and his grandmother, to take up the slack in his absence. Leaving the men wouldn't have kept him awake at night, but he couldn't give even a passing thought to leaving his seventy-eight-year-old grandmother to help finish moving the cattle to new grass, and then check a few fences before heading in, just so he could go back to the house and coax another kiss out of Emily.

So he clamped down on his impatience and tried to keep his mind on the task at hand, namely moving the cattle to fresh grass. He couldn't justify heading in for another couple of hours, at least. There were still fences to be checked, and, when they got back, tack to be repaired.

Rose rode up next to him. "I'm heading in for the day," she told him.

He eyed her critically. "Tired?"

She narrowed her eyes. "I can still outlast you all day in the saddle, Grandson, even at my age."

Sloan held up a hand. "Not saying any different. Just asking. You might not be tired, but I am."

"Ride back in with me. They don't need us for this. I want to talk to you."

Sloan bit back a groan. Invoices. She was going to want to talk about this month's invoices. Well, it couldn't be helped. The ranch was a business, and it was theirs. No one else was going to take care of it. But damn, he hated bookkeeping.

"Sure," he told her. "Let me tell the others, and I'll catch up with you."

Caleb was the nearest. Sloan rode over to him and

told him he was riding back to the house with their grandmother and he'd see the rest of them there when they came in for the day. Then he caught up with her.

He was glad she was going in. She talked a good game about being able to outlast him in the saddle, but she had no business spending all day on horseback at her age.

Of course, he was only a mortal man, so he would never say such a thing within her hearing. It had been many years since he'd had his ears boxed, and he wasn't fool enough to push his luck.

He slowed his horse to match her pace. "What did you want to talk about?"

"Windows."

"Pardon?" That certainly wasn't what he'd been expecting. "What windows?"

"The ones in our house. We have a lot of them, you know."

"And what? They need washing?"

"Oh, probably, but they're clean enough to see out of."

He hated it when she got cryptic. "And what have you seen out of our windows?" The instant the words were out, he knew.

"Lots of things. My bedroom windows, for instance, look out over the backyard, the garden. The creek."

"The creek."

"I've seen two cute little girls playing in the yard. That's a nice sight. The Cherokee Rose needs children."

Uh-oh, Sloan thought.

"I've seen a pretty woman with yellow hair working in our garden to bring food to our table. I've seen my eldest grandson kissing that pretty woman."

"Spying on me, Grandmother?"

"Ha!" She laughed. "You can't stand out in the open and expect privacy around here. You know better than that."

"Okay, so what's your point?"

She looked at him then for the first time since he'd caught up with her. "I just wonder if you know what you're doing."

Sloan couldn't hold her gaze for long because, in truth, he wasn't sure he did know what he was doing. "I'm just helping out a woman in need."

His grandmother's lips twitched. She looked away, faced forward again. "And she needs help with kissing?"

"You're either trying to make me laugh, or make me mad."

"Neither. She's a good woman."

Sloan was more than surprised at his grandmother's words. Rose generally liked people, but she tended to be stingy with her praise outside the family. "I'm glad you like her."

"I can see that you like her, too," Rose said. "That is good."

"Now don't start thinking there's more going on than there is."

"I have eyes. I see the way you look at her, when you stop fighting the need to fill your eyes."

He shook his head. "It doesn't matter what you see. She's only here long enough to get her car fixed and get back on the road to Arkansas."

"You're going to simply let her go?"

He looked at her, stunned. ''Of course I'm going to let her go. She's not mine to keep.''

Rose let out a long-suffering sigh. ''I suppose.''

''Come on, Grandmother, look at her. A woman that dainty and delicate wouldn't survive two months out here on the ranch. You don't want me falling for another helpless female, do you?''

''Of course I don't. But if you think Emily is helpless, then you need glasses, Grandson. She's a strong, competent woman.''

''I don't mean to say she's weak or incompetent. I don't mean that at all. It's just— Never mind. She'll be gone in a matter of days anyway, and that's the end of this conversation.''

Rose made a humming sound deep in her throat, but thankfully said no more on the subject. She questioned him instead on the condition of the hay crop, would they have enough stored to get them through winter if it was a hard one.

''With all this rain we've been getting, we'll have plenty,'' he assured her. And damn, but it felt good to be able to say that. Some years they had to truck hay in from some other state that hadn't been hit by a drought just to get the herd through the winter. Those years were a pure bitch.

When they reached the corral, Sloan swung down from his horse. After Rose dismounted he took her reins. As much as he wanted to rush to the house to see Emily, he knew his grandmother was tired, even if she wouldn't admit it.

''I'll see to your horse,'' he told her.

''Thank you, Grandson.'' She patted his cheek.

"I'm ready for a shower, and maybe even a nap, but if you repeat the latter, I'll deny it."

He blinked. "Repeat what?"

"You always were a good boy."

Since Rose was going to be in the house with Emily, Sloan decided it would be wise if he kept his distance. He wasn't ready for another lecture on the virtues of their temporary housekeeper. He feared he knew them all too well.

He wanted her.

There. He had actually let the words form in his brain. The big question was, what was he going to do about it?

While cooling down and grooming his mount and his grandmother's, he considered the possibilities.

The first was that Emily was not interested in anything beyond that one kiss they'd already shared. In which case, his wants were moot.

But she had said she was attracted to him, too. That meant something, didn't it? Of course it did. He could act on that, go after her. That's what he wanted to do. He remembered the day he met her, that slow, graceful dance she'd performed while gliding from table to table. Remembered wondering if she moved that slowly, that gracefully in bed. He still wondered it, and the wondering heated his blood.

Would it be worth it to have her, then stand back and watch her drive away?

And she would drive away. She would have to, because she wasn't cut out for life on a ranch. She had no business even being a housekeeper. Earline was as hefty as a linebacker, and the job wore her to a frazzle.

Memories of his mother surfaced, warm, loving,

sad. She'd been delicate and dainty, too, like Emily. And in the end, life on this ranch had killed her. He'd been nine, and devastated.

His mother, he knew, was why he always fell for damsels in distress. Women who needed him to help them. His mother had needed a man to help her through her daily life, but his father had been consumed by the ranch, and the bottle.

Sloan had stepped in to fill the void, but he'd been a kid. He hadn't been able to take care of his mother the way she needed, the way she deserved.

These days, it seemed, he made up for his youthful inabilities by helping any woman he thought needed him.

It was a hell of a thing, to realize all of that, and still fall in the same old trap. Because he could never, in good conscience, tie himself to a woman like his mother. He couldn't stand to watch a woman he loved work herself to the bone and wither away before his eyes. Would never forgive himself if he did that to a woman.

So what the hell was he even thinking of, to consider getting involved with Emily? She wasn't the type for a brief, hot fling. She had *home* and *hearth* written all over her.

Why couldn't he gravitate, just once in his life, toward *loose* and *wild?*

In the end Sloan dallied so long in the tack room in the barn that their two part-time men came and left for home, and his brothers rode in and beat him to the shower.

Everyone was just sitting down at the table by the time he'd gotten himself cleaned up and made it to the kitchen.

Janie and Libby were bubbling over, chomping at the bit to be able to tell everyone about their day.

"And then I fell and skinned my elbow. See my owie?" Libby held up the elbow for all to see.

"That's a beaut, all right," Justin said.

"Did it hurt?" Sloan asked.

"It was *awful,*" she said. "But then I forgot about it when the washing machine broke and water went everywhere. That was cool. But it was okay, because Miss Melanie was here to help Mommy take care of it."

Sloan inwardly winced. First because Emily had been confronted with a problem she shouldn't have had to deal with. Second, "Mel was here?"

Emily passed the sliced tomatoes to Rose. "You call her Mel?"

He shrugged. "Sometimes. Is the washer okay now, or do we need to take a look at it?"

"No, it's fine. It just needed a new hose for the cold water."

Rose took a slice of tomato and passed the plate along. "I thought the porch floor looked unusually clean."

Emily smiled. "Oh, it got a good mopping, all right."

Sloan told himself it was no big deal that Mel had to replace the hose while she was here. Most women didn't know squat about plumbing; Mel was the exception. He couldn't think less of Emily for needing the help. He doubted his grandmother could have handled it on her own, and she could do damn near anything, although she tended to turn her nose up at plumbing.

"Men's work," she had always said. "Plumbing

and electricity and car engines.'' Anything else, to her way of thinking, was fair game, but women shouldn't be bothered by any of those three pesky chores. Scrubbing toilets, she'd said, was bad enough.

No, he shouldn't feel disappointed that Emily had needed Mel's help. He was only sorry that he hadn't been here himself to take care of the problem for her.

''What did Melanie want?'' Caleb asked Emily.

''She brought dessert.''

''No fooling?'' Justin straightened and looked around the room. ''What'd she bring?''

''Listen to you,'' Rose scolded. ''You sound like you never get dessert. And after that wonderful banana pudding Emily made yesterday.''

Emily took no offense at Justin's remark. ''She said their blackberries were out of control. She brought pies.''

''Awright,'' Justin cried. ''Hot? With ice cream?''

Sloan snorted. ''Heat your own pie. Emily doesn't need to be doing extra work like heating a piece of pie for a nitwit. Next thing, you'll be asking her to cut your meat and tie your shoes.''

Justin winked at Emily. ''Don't mind him. He's probably just worried about whatever Mel might have told you about him.''

Sloan nearly choked on a sip of iced tea.

Emily grinned. ''You mean like the fact that she had a bad crush on him for most of her life?''

Sloan's face turned an interesting shade of red.

Justin chuckled. ''That's our Mel.''

''Did you run a count when we moved those cattle?'' Maybe changing the subject, Sloan thought, would save him the serious razzing he feared was coming.

''Sixty-three,'' Justin replied, ''all present and accounted for.''

''You're sure. We didn't miss any down in that draw?''

''We didn't miss any. I counted two-hundred-and-fifty-two legs, and divided by four.''

''Not without a calculator, you didn't,'' Sloan taunted. ''Math never was your strong suit.''

''Hey,'' Justin protested. ''I can count just fine.''

''I seem to remember a D in math your junior year in high school.''

''Yes,'' Caleb joined in. ''I remember that, too. But be fair, Sloan. That D had nothing to do with his inability to add or subtract, but with the fact that Beverly Anniston of the tight-fitting, low-necked sweaters sat beside him.'' He grinned. ''Speaking of Ds.''

''That's right,'' Justin proclaimed. ''How's a guy supposed to concentrate with all that—''

''Watch out, Grandson,'' Rose warned, a twinkle in her eye as she used her fork to cut a piece from her tomato slice.

''I was going to say *distraction,*'' Justin claimed.

''How very diplomatic of you,'' his grandmother said.

Chapter Seven

"It occurs to me," Sloan said to Emily after supper, "that you've been here several days and we haven't got you or your girls up on horseback yet. Most kids would have been clamoring for a ride by now. Don't they like horses?"

Emily gave the kitchen countertop a final swipe with the dishrag. "They've never been around horses before."

"Meaning?"

She draped the wet dishrag over the sink divider and turned to face him. "Meaning I think they're probably dying to ride, but because I told them not to ask, they haven't."

Sloan's eyes widened. "Why would you tell them not to ask? Kids, horses, wide-open spaces, it's a no-brainer."

She gave him a small, tight smile. "For summer

camp, maybe. But we're not here for a vacation, we're here for me to work. I didn't think it was appropriate."

"Well, stuff that." He took her by the hand and headed for the back door. "Here to work," he muttered. "What do you think this is, the salt mines?"

Janie held her little sister's hand tightly. The two of them stood well back from the garage, as ordered. Mr. Caleb and Mr. Justin had brought in this big thing they called an A-frame and stood it over the car engine. Now they had huge, long chains, as big around as Janie's arm, hanging from the crossbar. The other ends of the chains were hooked onto the engine, and they were turning this handle thing, like a crank, and lifting the engine up. They said they weren't going to pull it clear up in the air, just high enough that they could get to that thing underneath that they needed to get to. Something called an oil pan, she thought. Whatever that was.

"Golly," Libby said beside her, her eyes wide.

Janie squeezed Libby's hand. It was kind of scary, what the men were doing. Mr. Justin said she and Libby had to stand way back out of the way in case something broke and the engine fell.

"That big ol' thing would squash you like a bug, and we sure don't want that to happen," he'd said.

Half of what Mr. Justin said, Janie knew, was teasing. But this time, she believed him.

"We have to do something," Janie murmured.

"What do you mean?" Libby asked.

"About the car." She pushed her glasses up on her nose. "If Mr. Caleb fixes the car, we'll have to leave and go to Fort Smith."

''We can't leave,'' Libby protested. ''What about the survey? Mr. Sloan has to be our new daddy.''

''Shh. I know. That's why we have to do something.''

But what could they do? Janie wondered as she watched the two men point and gesture toward the engine. Mr. Caleb would repair whatever was wrong with the car, then put it back together, and it would be fixed.

Then an idea occurred to her. It made her heart pound and her hands got slick with sweat. ''I know what we'll do,'' she whispered.

''What?'' Libby whispered back.

''Shh. They might hear us, and it has to be a secret.''

After dragging Emily out of the house Sloan spotted the girls watching Caleb and Justin pull the car engine. He should have been out here helping them, but, damn it, some things—like talking with Emily—were more important than helping fix the car that would take her away from him.

''There they are,'' he said unnecessarily. ''Hey, girls, whatcha doing?''

''Look.'' Libby pointed at the A-frame standing over the car.

''Oh, my.'' Emily stared. ''Well, that's progress.''

''Yes,'' Sloan murmured, none too pleased with the idea. Then, with a sigh, he strode toward his brothers. ''If you'd told me you were doing this now, I'd have helped.''

''Did we say we needed any help?'' Caleb asked.

''No, as a matter of fact,'' Sloan admitted, his good mood restored. ''You didn't. We're out of here.

Ladies, if you please.'' He swept his arm toward the barn and corrals.

Libby gave a little hop and skip. ''Where we goin'?''

''Oh,'' he said casually. ''I don't know. Maybe we'll go saddle up a horse and ride around for a while.''

Libby squealed and clapped her hands.

Janie sucked in a sharp breath, her eyes widening. ''Really? A horseback ride?''

''Would you like that?'' Sloan asked, with a quick wink at Emily.

''Yes, sir!''

''You guys have fun,'' Sloan called to his brothers. ''We're going riding.''

''They're naturals,'' Rose said. ''Both of them.'' She had come out to watch and now stood beside Emily at the corral fence watching Sloan lead their gentlest mare, Suzie Q, around the corral. Janie and Libby grinned from astride the mare's bare back.

''This is the thrill of their lives,'' Emily said. She could clearly remember the thrill of her first childhood horseback ride, of feeling as if she were the tallest person in the world while she was up there on the back of that magnificent steed.

She hadn't cared that that magnificent steed was a thirty-year-old nag who refused to move at any pace faster than cold molasses. She'd been *riding.* On a *horse.*

She'd been seven, and Michael had made it all possible, since the horse belonged to his cousin. If she hadn't already been in love with him, she would have fallen for him that day.

"Look, Mommy, look at us!" Libby called.

"I see you," Emily called back. "You look wonderful, both of you. How does it feel?"

"I'm so tall," she crowed.

Emily laughed, so grateful to Sloan for this moment, for suggesting it. She wanted her daughters to ride horses, swing on old tire swings, suck on lollipops. She wanted them to have a happy, normal childhood. Leaving Pueblo had been the first step toward that goal, away from the sadness of the past, away from struggling to put food on the table.

This interlude at the Cherokee Rose, with Sloan and his family, was something her girls would always remember, and something for which Emily would always be grateful.

"I don't know who's having more fun," Rose said. "The girls or Sloan."

It was true, Emily realized. She'd been so focused on Janie and Libby that she hadn't noticed the look of sheer pleasure on Sloan's face. He should have children, she thought. He would be such a good father, with his kindness and patience and good humor.

After a few more minutes Sloan lifted each of the girls down, then came to stand before Emily. "Your turn," he said.

Emily smiled. "All right, but I want a saddle."

"Have you ever ridden?"

"Yes, but it's been years and years ago. I think Suzie Q here is just about my speed."

"With a saddle."

"Yes, please."

"Mommy, mommy!"

"Mother, it was so fun!" Janie's face glowed with excitement.

Emily's heart clenched. *Thank you, Sloan, for putting that look on my oh-so-serious daughter's face.* Emily put an arm around each girl and hugged them both. "I'm so glad you liked it."

"When can we do it again?" Libby wanted to know.

Emily laughed. "I don't know. We'll see."

"Did you see, Miss Rose?" the little one asked. "We rode a horse."

"I saw. You looked good up there. We'll make horsewomen out of you two yet."

Libby scrunched up her face. "What's a horse swimmin'?"

Rose laughed. "Horse women. Women who ride horses."

"Oh. But we're not women, we're just little girls. Can we be cowgirls?"

Emily wasn't sure how it had happened, but Sloan had brought Suzie Q to her, saddled and ready to ride, and she'd ridden her around the corral. He'd pronounced her proficient enough for a trip through the pasture to the north pond—wherever that was—and Rose asked if she could give the girls ice cream to celebrate their ride. Now, here Emily was, riding across the grassy acres with Sloan riding next to her, the evening sun in her eyes, the south wind in her hair. He kept the horses to a walk, which she greatly appreciated.

She looked over at Sloan and found him watching her, a small smile on his lips. "Thank you," she told him.

He looked surprised. "For what?"

"For this. I haven't ridden since I was a kid. I love

it. And for the girls. You're their hero now. Thank you for giving them this evening."

"Your girls." He let out a breath and shook his head slightly, as if in wonder. "They're so special, Emily. It's a real kick to see the world through their eyes. A privilege to be part of their world. I'm the one who should be thanking you, for sharing them with me."

Emily sniffed. "You're trying to make me cry."

He looked so suddenly horrified that she laughed.

Then he looked sheepish. "I'm trying to make you like me. Not that I didn't mean what I said—I meant every word of it."

"Sloan, I already like you."

He gave her an exaggerated leer. "You do?"

She laughed again. "I'm not saying another word. Where are we going?"

"Just over this rise we'll turn north toward the pond. It's a pretty spot. I thought you might like it."

How could she not like it? she thought. The greens in their varying shades were so vivid, from the dark oak leaves to the blue-green of the grass to the emerald of the cottonwoods and the paler shade of the narrow willow leaves. The sky was a sharp, breathless blue. The wind was a warm caress. It was all like a dream.

Then there was the man at her side, whose lips had touched hers. Would he try to kiss her again? Would she let him?

Ha. Let him? If he didn't make a move soon, she thought she might just beg him.

They topped the low rise and the land stretched out ahead of them forever toward the lowering sun. Sloan angled them to the right toward a gleaming spot of water surrounded by a thin scattering of trees. The pond was maybe a half acre in size. As they rode near, a dozen or more mallard ducks flapped their wings and, with a flutter of noise, lifted toward the sky.

Emily nudged her horse to follow Sloan to the shade of a towering cottonwood beside the pond.

"Stay put," he said as he swung down from the saddle. "I'll help you down."

"That's all right." Shifting her weight into the left stirrup, she swung her right leg over the back of the horse and slid to the ground. Right into Sloan's waiting arms.

"I said I'd help." His voice, as well as his arms, wrapped around her from behind.

For an instant, Emily melted. This was what she had wanted, wasn't it? From the moment he'd kissed her, she had wanted to feel his touch, his nearness again. Wanted to find out if she had only imagined the warm tingling sensation deep inside, the goose-flesh on her arms.

She hadn't imagined it. It was real, all of it, and it swamped her again. And this, from only his arms touching hers, his breath brushing the back of her neck.

For the life of her, she couldn't remember what he'd just said to her.

"You said you would think about it." This time the warmth of his breath brushed across her ear.

She shuddered. In pure delight. There was no use pretending she didn't know what he was talking about. He'd said he would want to kiss her again, and she'd said she would think about it.

"Have you?" He ran his hands up her arms to her

shoulders and turned her to face him. She was trapped between his broad chest and her horse. ‘‘Have you thought about it?’’

Only in her sleep, and every waking moment. The guilt. The thrill. ‘‘Yes.’’

‘‘And?’’ He leaned closer, his face so near it consumed her vision.

She leaned toward him. ‘‘And.’’

He didn’t wait for a verbal invitation. He slid his arms around her and took her mouth with his.

This wasn’t the gentle brush of lips like the last time. This was a taking. She reveled in it and gave back, measure for measure. With her mouth on his, she ran her hands up his hard, muscled arms, over his broad shoulders, to his neck. She threaded her fingers into his thick, soft hair. Oh, the feel of it against the sensitive skin between her fingers. Who would have thought that simply touching a man’s hair could make her spine tingle this way?

It had been so long since a man had held her. So incredibly long since she had felt this familiar heat in her blood. Was it wrong to take this pleasure? It couldn’t be. She wouldn’t let it be. She sank into the kiss, into the man, and lost herself to the sheer wonder of it. His tongue was like hot velvet against hers.

Her hands found their way down his arms again, then up, across his chest. Fascinated, she followed the dips and hollows of hard muscles. She’d never felt such strength in a man before. She wanted to feel his skin. Would it be smooth or rough, hot or cool?

She caught herself starting to open a snap and jerked back.

Sloan blinked, shook his head to clear it. ‘‘What?’’ His breath was coming hard. ‘‘What’s wrong?’’

She looked up at him with those sky-blue eyes and swallowed. "Nothing."

But something was. She had jerked away as if he had suddenly burst into flames. Hell, he damn near had.

Then he realized where her hands had been, what they'd been doing just before she'd broken off that mind-numbing kiss. He chuckled, if a little breathlessly. "Hey, it's all right with me if you want to unsnap my shirt."

Her face turned the prettiest shade of red he thought he'd ever seen. She sucked in a sharp breath and took a step back. And ran up against the horse.

Suzie Q snorted and sidestepped away from Emily, leaving Emily with no support, throwing her off balance. Her eyes widened as she started to tumble.

Sloan snared her by the arms before she could fall and pulled her to his chest. "I've got you."

Despite her acute embarrassment, Emily laughed. "That was spoken with entirely too much confidence to suit me."

"What?" He grinned down at her and ran his hands up and down her back while pressing her against his chest. "That I've got you?" He couldn't get enough of the smell of her, something light and flowery. He could easily become addicted to the feel of her breasts against him. "Maybe it's wishful thinking."

"It's nice thinking," she said shyly.

"Yeah?"

"Yes." She slipped out of his arms and turned to stroke Suzie Q between the eyes. "But it's pointless, you know."

"I like you, you like me. What's pointless about that?"

She gave the horse a final pat, then walked toward the pond. Sloan followed her as if he were a puppy on a leash. But what else could a man do, he thought.

"I'm only here until my car's fixed," she reminded him.

He hadn't needed the reminder.

"Judging by the progress Caleb is making, that should only be a couple more days. A few days after that I'll have earned enough to pay for the repairs, and a couple more days I'll have enough to pay you for towing my car from New Mexico."

"Now, hold on," he protested. "You're not paying me for towing your car."

"That's not my point."

"I mean it," he said, stopping next to her at the edge of the reddish-brown water. "Towing your car was like bringing your suitcase along. That's all. No charge."

"My point," she said, lips pursed, "is that I'll be gone in a few days."

He gave her a wry smile. "You never heard of making hay while the sun shines?"

She chuckled.

"Hey, that's a saying we take seriously around here."

"That's fine," she told him. "As long as it's hay you're talking about."

Sloan reached out and took her hand. "You don't believe in living for the moment? Grabbing for what you can while it's there?" He tugged her closer, nuzzled the side of her face. "When it's something you want clear down to your toes?"

Emily could feel herself melting at his low, seductive tone. Another minute and she would be in his arms again. And would that be so wrong?

"Just because you leave the ranch doesn't mean we can't still see each other, if we want to."

"Oh, sure, you're going to drive to Arkansas to take me out to dinner and a movie."

"I don't have a problem with that. Do you?"

Emily chuckled. "Is this what they call a one-track mind?"

"Ah, come on. Give a guy a break."

She pulled her hand from his grasp. "Give a guy a break and do what, have sex with him because he wants me to?"

Sloan raised his hands in surrender. "Okay, I give. I take it all back. If you'd rather, I'll go back to ignoring you."

Emily's heart sank. "You're angry."

He let out a gust of breath. "That's an understatement. But at myself, not you. I obviously managed to make this sound, I don't know, tawdry. That's not how I meant it at all. And, okay, I'm a little mad at you for taking it all wrong. I thought we might have something going here. I thought it was mutual."

Disheartened, disgusted with herself, Emily sat on the grass and hugged her knees. "I'm sorry." She couldn't look at him. "I'm no good at this."

He lowered himself to the grass beside her. "No good at what?"

She shrugged and pulled a blade of grass through her fingers. "This man-woman stuff. I've never played this game before."

"Is that what you think I'm doing? Playing a game?" Sloan was losing her, he knew. He could feel her slipping right through his grasp. Not that she'd ever been his to lose, but he'd had his hopes. Was he simply being perverse? Telling himself he wanted her, while chalking up a list of all the reasons they were wrong for each other?

Reasons. One, really. She wasn't suited to life on a ranch. Now he had to figure that she wasn't suited to life with him.

Life? God, if she could hear his thoughts. She assumed he wanted a roll in the hay and nothing more, and the word *life* kept zipping through his mind.

"I honestly don't know," she said in answer to his question. "I only know that I'm here for a matter of days, no more, and you seem to want something from me I don't think I'm prepared to give."

Hope was a funny thing, Sloan thought. It sprang to life at the slightest provocation. He reached toward her, and with the tip of his index finger beneath her chin, turned her face toward his. "I don't want to *take* anything from you, Em, I just thought, if you wanted to, we could get together, pass a little mutually satisfying time together, and see where it leads."

Her cheeks were as pink as the streaks cast across the sky by the setting sun. "I told you I wasn't any good at this sort of stuff. I like you, Sloan. I am attracted to you. I just don't know what, if anything, I should do about it."

"There's no *should* to it," he said gently. "You either feel like getting closer to me, or you don't. I'm a big boy, Em. I can take rejection. Not well," he added with a quirk of his lips, "but I can take it. I guess I've been rushing you, and I apologize for that. Come on, let's head back before it gets dark."

* * *

That night Emily lay awake for hours going over in her head every gesture they'd made, every word they'd spoken at the pond. She'd made such a mess of it, she felt like an inexperienced fool.

At the thought, she bit back a laugh. She wasn't ready to admit to the fool part, but, mother of two children or not, she was inexperienced when it came to dealing with men. The only man she'd ever had anything to do with was Michael.

Wanting Sloan felt like a betrayal of everything she and Michael had shared. The guilt gnawed at her.

But that was unreasonable. Michael had been gone for two years now, and she'd been alone. He had loved her every bit as much as she had loved him. He would want her to find someone new. Wouldn't he?

She tried to think in the reverse—if she had died and left Michael alone. Wouldn't she want him to be happy? Or was she so petty that she would prefer he spend the rest of his life pining for her?

Oh, heaven above, she hoped what was inside her was the former. Thinking she might be small and petty didn't sit well with her. Michael would be ashamed of her for such thoughts.

Michael is dead.

Yes, he was dead. Gone. But never forgotten. He was and always would be alive in her heart, and she did her best to keep him alive for his daughters.

Oh, Michael, what am I going to do?

Heaven help her, was she actually asking her husband if she should give in to her desire and make love with Sloan?

Emily, girl, that's just sick.

But in the darkness of the room she shared with

her daughters, Michael's daughters, she smiled up at the ceiling. She could see him getting a good belly laugh from the irony of it all.

Sloan, too, had trouble sleeping that night. He told himself until the wee hours of the morning that he was wasting his time chasing after Emily. She was right. What was the point? She'd be leaving in a few days. And since his suggestion that he could drive to Fort Smith to take her out had been met with a decided lack of enthusiasm—or belief—that, it seemed, would be that. No point in beating his head, or his heart—

His heart? When had that pathetic organ chimed in on the situation?

Bleary-eyed, he climbed out of bed the same time he did every morning. He didn't need an alarm to tell him it was time to get to work. The rooster had been crowing for more than an hour. The sun would be up soon.

He didn't know what he expected from Emily when he went downstairs for breakfast after he'd showered and shaved and grunted a time or two at his brothers, but the possibility of a cold shoulder had crossed his mind. He was grateful to beat the rest of the family to the kitchen.

Emily was alone in the kitchen, working on her second skilletful of bacon, when she heard a sound behind her. Startled, she whirled. Her hand passed over the skillet just as a slice of bacon gave up a drop of moisture and sent grease popping across her palm. She yelped and grabbed her burned hand.

Sloan rushed to her side. ''You hurt yourself.''

With little sleep the night before, Emily was not in

the best of moods. She stepped around him and thrust her hand under a stream of cold water at the sink.

"No," she told him. "I didn't do anything to myself. You snuck up on me, startled me, and grease popped on my hand."

"I'm sorry," Sloan said. "I didn't mean to startle you."

"No." She let out a sigh. The cold water felt good on her palm. "I know you didn't. I'm sorry. There was no need for me to snap at you." She turned off the water and reached for a dish towel.

"Let me see." Sloan took her hand and cupped it in his palm. Three red spots decorated the center of it. "We've got a tube of something for burns."

"Yes, I'll get it later." His hands, warm against hers, tempted her to linger. She made a move to pull away.

He held on. "You didn't get any blisters yesterday from riding, did you?"

"No, no blisters."

His thumb traced lightly across her palm, sending a shiver down her spine.

"I should have found you a pair of gloves."

Her lips quirked. She pulled free of his light grasp and stepped back to the stove. "You should have found me a thick pillow. It's not my hands that suffered."

Sloan chuckled, but the sound was filled with sympathy. "We have a tub of something for that, too."

"I've already used it," she confessed with a laugh. With a long turning fork she lifted the final strips of bacon from the skillet and placed them on a paper towel to drain.

"Em, about yesterday."

She wasn't sure she was ready to talk about yesterday yet. She turned off the flame beneath the skillet and moved it to a cold burner.

"I only meant to take you for a ride," he offered.

She gave him a look from the corner of her eye.

"Make that, horseback ride," he corrected. "I didn't take you out to the pond with the plan to get you into bed. Or the grass, as the case may be."

"If I'd thought that's what you were after, I wouldn't have gone with you."

"I just wanted to, I don't know, show you around the place a little. I thought you'd enjoy going riding. I wasn't thinking about getting your clothes off. Well, I mean, I wasn't planning on it."

A bark of laughter escaped her.

"Yeah," he said. "Well, I'm trying to be honest here. I haven't talked so much like this to a woman in, well, ever. I want you to know the truth. I thought maybe we could—do they still use the word *neck?*"

Emily laughed again at the red stain creeping up his neck. "That'll do. And we did, didn't we? I mean, a little bit."

"So, does this mean you're not mad at me?"

She gave him a smile and a slice of crisp bacon. "I'm not mad, Sloan."

He took the bacon with one hand and stroked her cheek with the other. "You look like you didn't get much sleep."

"Well, now I'm mad," she said tartly. "No woman likes to hear that."

Chapter Eight

Since Caleb had been doing all the work on Emily's car in the evenings, Justin figured he'd give the guy a break and change the oil in the tractor himself before it was time to cut hay again. But the oil wasn't in the tractor shed, it was down in the garage. He strolled along past the corrals and barn and enjoyed the sunshine and the hot south wind.

A flash of pink at the open garage door alerted him. He slowed, then paused. Whispering. The funny thing about whispering was that the sibilant hiss of it tended to carry farther than normally spoken words. The only reasons to whisper, in Justin's experience, were when you didn't want anyone to hear what you were saying to your sweetheart, or when you were saying something you knew you weren't supposed to say.

Quietly he walked to the garage door and leaned against it.

Janie was gathering up nuts and bolts in her small hands. ''He'll need these to put the car back together. If he can't find them, he can't finish the car, and we won't have to leave and go to Fort Smith.''

''But that's stealing,'' Libby whispered back.

''It is not. It's our car, isn't it? So these things are ours, too. You can't steal from yourself.''

Justin bit back a chuckle. Smart little cookie, that Janie. It sounded to him as if she and her sister were in no hurry to continue on their way to Arkansas. He figured maybe they had the right idea.

''Hiya, girls,'' he said. ''Whatcha doin'?''

Both girls jerked and squeaked. Never had guilt been so blatantly stamped on such pretty little faces.

''Nothing,'' they said in unison.

''I just came down here to get some oil for the tractor. Would you look at that mess?'' He pointed to the oil-stained tarp Caleb had spread out beneath the front end of the car. On it lay all the nuts and bolts and various parts that he had taken from the engine.

Justin shook his head in mock dismay. ''Something's gonna get lost if Caleb leaves that stuff lying around like that.'' He squatted down next to the girls and picked up a bolt. ''Of course, it won't matter much if these nuts and bolts and screws and stuff get lost. We've got a zillion of them around here we can use to replace them. But this little thing here,'' he added, nudging with his index finger the oil pickup tube Caleb had removed and cleaned last night. ''This thing gets kicked around and accidentally lost, why, no telling how long it might take to replace it.''

Janie blinked up at him, all serious and wide-eyed, her mind running a mile a minute or his name wasn't Justin Chisholm. ''How come?'' she asked.

"Are you kidding? A car this old, nobody keeps a part like that lying around. There's probably not another one of these little tubes for this particular vehicle for fifty miles. Maybe a hundred. Could take a week or two to track down a replacement and get it shipped in."

"It could?" Janie darted a quick look at Libby.

"It sure could." He pushed himself to his feet and shook his head. "Caleb needs to be more careful with stuff. I'll have to tell him to do just that, next time I see him."

Janie swallowed and craned her neck to look up at him. "When might that be?"

"Oh, probably not 'til suppertime tonight. Now, if you ladies will excuse me, I better get that oil and get back down to the tractor. We'll be wanting to cut hay probably next week, and I don't want to leave this for the last minute."

Whistling as if he didn't have a care in the world, Justin took the oil he needed from the cabinet in the back, grabbed the spout and funnel and sauntered back out of the garage. "See you girls later."

"'Bye, Mr. Justin," Libby called.

It was all he could do to keep from laughing out loud all the way back to the tractor.

Oh, he did like a devious mind. He wondered where they would hide the oil pickup tube. Wondered if he was going to be able to keep a straight face when Caleb tore the garage apart looking for it.

Sloan made it back to the barn in the middle of the afternoon and was pleased to learn that Justin had changed the oil in the tractor. It was due, and then some.

"We'll be needing this sucker in a few days, maybe a week," he said.

"The hay's nearly ready?"

"Yep. This rain we've been getting has helped. If we could get another good soaking in the next day or two, then a good dry spell, it'll be damn near perfect."

Justin wiped his hands on an oily rag. "It's turning out to be a good year."

Sloan looked out and surveyed the only home any of them had ever known. Two little girls played and giggled in the backyard and a pretty blond-headed lady knelt in the garden. "It sure is." Now, he thought with a heavy feeling in the pit of his stomach, if only it was real.

Oh, the hay was real enough. And it was true that the weather had been their friend this year, for which he remembered to give thanks, because it was a rare thing. Normally the rains came at the worst possible time, followed by weeks of drought, or an early freeze, or a late one, or a tornado.

And the family, that was real enough to be thankful for, too.

It was the woman and the children that weren't real. Weren't his.

And they shouldn't be, he told himself. He wished he could stop pulling himself in opposite directions over Emily. His head kept telling him she wasn't cut out for life on a ranch. She would end up pale and rundown and wasted, like his mother, and that would kill him. And maybe her, too. His head also told him that if she continued to need his help every time he turned around, he would get tired of it.

But his heart argued that she was the woman he'd been waiting to meet his entire life. He had to admire a woman who could raise two such terrific kids. And she wasn't that helpless, was she?

Or maybe, he thought wryly, it wasn't his heart, but an area farther south that kept ignoring his head and wanting her when he knew he shouldn't. He wanted to hold her, touch her, taste her. He wanted to feel her flesh against his.

And she was having none of it.

Maybe it was for the best.

"What's the matter with you?" Justin nudged his shoulder. "You look like somebody just ran over your favorite puppy."

The sound that came from Sloan's throat sounded suspiciously like a growl.

"She gets to you, huh?"

Sloan turned away. From his brother, from the view of Emily and the girls. "I don't know what you're talking about."

"Ha! Who are you trying to kid, me? Or yourself?"

"When's the last time anybody told you to shut up?"

"I don't know what your problem is. She seems perfect for you. What are you going to do, let her slip right through your fingers?"

"Butt out, kid."

Justin threw his hands in the air. "Butting out. Butting way out."

Sloan opened his mouth to have another go at him, because griping at Justin was easier than thinking about Emily, but he was cut off by the scream of a little girl.

* * *

Emily was taking a break from housework to spend some time in Rose's vegetable garden. She'd brought a plastic five-gallon bucket with her to collect the day's offering of tomatoes, squash, green beans and cucumbers. They'd be having fresh salad tonight for sure.

With half her mind on picking vegetables and pulling weeds and the other half on the girls playing on the other side of the fence in the backyard, the small gray snake startled her. She jerked back, then laughed at herself. It was just a little bug-eater, a gardener's friend. But at her sudden movement, it slithered under cover among the thick growth of bush beans.

Libby came over and draped herself against the chain-link fence. "Whatcha doin', Mommy?"

"I found a friend," Emily said. "You and Janie want to come see?"

"Janie, come see what Mommy found."

In seconds the girls had joined her in the garden, hunkered down with her between two rows of beans.

"What is it?" Janie asked, trying to peer around her mother while Libby sidled up and stood in front of Emily.

Emily studied the bases of the bean plants carefully. "I think he's hiding. He's probably scared of us. He's just a little guy."

"But what is it, Mother?" Janie asked.

"It's a snake," Emily told her. "A little gray snake."

"Snake?" Libby screamed at the top of her lungs. "Snake! It's a snake!" She bolted from the ground and rammed into Emily.

With Janie directly behind her, Emily lost her balance and did an awkward side flip over the row of beans. She barely had time to register the fact that she was facedown in the dirt, with a cucumber in her ear, when Libby was all over her, shrieking for all she was worth.

Heavy footfalls thundered toward the garden from across the drive.

"Emily!" Sloan leaped the two rows of bush beans to land next to her.

While Janie called her sister's name, Libby's shrieks subsided into pitiful sobs.

"What's wrong?" Sloan demanded frantically. "Em? Libby? Are you all right? What happened?"

"Libby, baby," Emily groaned. "Get off me, baby."

"I've got her." Sloan lifted Libby in his arms and started wiping her tears. "Are you hurt, sweetie?"

Sniff, sniff. "No, I was scared."

"Em?" he asked. "Are you okay?"

With another groan, Emily pushed herself to her knees. "I'm okay. Just in shock."

"What happened?" he demanded.

"I don't know. Libby, why did you scream, baby?"

Libby sniffed again. "You said it was a snake."

"A snake?" Sloan practically jerked Emily to her feet. "Where? Did it get you?"

"Relax," Emily said, half amused, half irritated. "It was just a little gray bug-eater. Libby, you weren't afraid of snakes last summer when we went up in the hills and had the picnic for Carol Ann's birthday party." She took Libby from Sloan's arms and stood her on the ground. Kneeling before her youngest, she used the hem of her T-shirt to mop the girl's face. As her shirt now had garden soil ground into it, Libby's face became a mess.

"Remember?" Emily said. "You found that little green snake and picked it up? You said it was cute and you carried it in your pocket."

Libby sniffed again. "I forgot."

"You forgot you weren't afraid of snakes?"

Libby's lower lip wobbled. "I was scared it might be a tobra."

Emily frowned. "A what?"

"A tobra." *Sniff.* "Like comes out of the basket on TV."

"I don't..." Emily looked questioningly at Sloan, who shook his head. At Justin, who shrugged. At Janie, who stared at the ground and dug the toe of her shoe in the dirt.

"Janie, do you know what she's talking about?"

Janie shrugged and twisted back and forth as if swaying in the wind. "Maybe."

"Maybe?"

Another shrug. "I guess."

"Janie," Emily said firmly. "Tell me."

Janie dared a look at her mother, then looked up at Sloan, then Justin, with a plea in her eyes. When neither man offered any help, she let out a dramatic sigh. "She means a cobra. We saw it on TV."

The light dawned. "And it comes out of a basket," Emily said. "A snake charmer."

"And it was great big and scary." Libby's voice shook. "And they said it kilt people. It gave me bad dreams. I told her it scared me, but she wouldn't change the channel. She called me a sissy.''

''I didn't *call* you a sissy, I told you not to *be* a sissy.''

''I'm not a sissy.'' Libby stuck out her tongue.

''Are, too.''

''All right, girls,'' Emily said sternly, ''that's enough. Let's go in the house and get cleaned up. Sloan, Justin, thank you for running to our rescue, so to speak. I'm sorry for all the commotion.''

At a complete loss, Sloan tagged along behind them until they disappeared inside the house. He stood in the dirt and stared at the back door, feeling shut out of his own house.

''Man,'' Justin said, standing beside him. ''Hearing a little girl scream like that, seeing Emily pitch face first to the ground. That'll take the starch out of a man's knees.''

''No fooling,'' Sloan said with feeling. In about a week, he was sure, his hands might stop shaking.

They just stood there for a couple of minutes. Sloan's mind was blank. Just...blank. Except for the echo of Libby's scream, the picture of Emily falling.

''So,'' Justin finally said. ''What do you think?''

Sloan let out a long breath and scrubbed a hand down his face. ''I think I need a beer.''

In the house, Emily washed all three of them up at the bathroom sink. She was in need of it worse than the girls. When they were all clean she took the girls to their bedroom and sat between them on the edge of her bed.

''Well,'' she said. ''That was exciting.''

Libby giggled. Couldn't keep her baby down for long, Emily thought, relieved. She smoothed her hand over Libby's hair. ''Are you okay now?''

She sniffed and nodded. ''I didn't think about a little snake. I just thought about the big, mean tobra.''

''Cobra,'' Janie corrected.

Emily put her arm around Janie. ''I think you owe somebody an apology, young lady.''

Janie hung her head. ''I'm sorry, Mommy.''

Emily's heart clenched. Janie hadn't called her that since Michael died. Since the day after the funeral she had called her Mother. ''I know you are, honey, but I'm not the one you need to apologize to.''

Janie mumbled something Emily couldn't make out.

''I didn't hear you.''

''I said, I know.''

''And?''

Janie peered over at her sister. ''I'm sorry, Lib. I didn't think it would scare you that bad.''

''Well, it did.'' Libby was going to milk this.

''Libby, when someone admits they did something wrong and apologizes, the correct response is, thank you. Apology accepted. And then you let it go and don't argue about it anymore.''

Now Libby hung her head. ''Okay.''

''Okay, what?''

''Okay, thank you, Janie.''

''Apology accepted,'' Emily prompted.

''Apology accepted.''

It wasn't the most gracious acceptance Emily had ever heard, but it would do.

Emily decided that after the emotional upheaval of the day, the girls had earned themselves a nap. They didn't much care for the idea; they would rather go back outside and play, as long, Libby said, as there weren't any tobras around. Emily assured her that there were no tobras, or cobras, either, anywhere in the entire country. But Libby needed to rest and regroup, and Janie had earned a little time-out.

"And I mean nap," she warned. "No TV for at least thirty minutes."

The latter might have been taken more seriously if she hadn't winked at them when she closed the bedroom door as she left.

She found Justin at the desk talking on the phone. She busied herself in the kitchen until he finished the call, then asked him where Sloan was.

"He's out at the barn," he said.

She hesitated, then asked. "Are you going to be in the house for a few minutes?"

"Yeah. I got stuck with dealing with an invoice screwup at the feed store."

"I hate to ask, but I need to talk to Sloan. Would you mind keeping an ear out for the girls? They're supposed to be napping, but if they turn on the television, that's okay. I just don't like leaving them alone in the house."

"No problem," he said easily. "Take your time. I'll be at this for at least an hour, at the rate things are going," he added with disgust.

"You're sure you don't mind?"

Justin chuckled to himself. Mind? "Of course not." Especially if it would help throw Emily and Sloan together, he thought. "Go easy on him. Little Libby screaming like that kinda shook him up. If you've got any of that incredible patience and sympathy left, he could probably use some about now."

He was grinning as he watched her rush out the door.

Sloan had barely finished his beer and had yet to settle his nerves before Melanie Pruitt pulled up at the barn where he was working.

He and Mel went way back, to childhood. He had always been uneasy around her, with that hard case of hero-worship she'd had for him for years. But lately, the past couple of years, she'd finally decided he was never going to see her as anything other than an honorary sister, and they had become friends. Good friends.

She sauntered toward him now with a swing in her hips and a cocky grin on her lips. "Hey, big guy."

"Mel." He waited for her to join him inside the barn, out of the sun. "What's up?"

"I was on my way to town and decided to stop at the last minute and see if Emily or Rose needed anything or wanted to go with me."

"That was nice of you, considering you never stop and invite any of us to ride to town with you."

"Hey, so sue me. I like Emily. I gotta say, Sloan, I didn't think you had it in you."

"Had what in me?"

"The ability to finally find the right woman."

Sloan was glad he had already finished his beer. If he'd had a mouthful just then he would have choked on it. "Pardon?"

Melanie leaned toward his face. "Em-i-ly," she

pronounced carefully. "You did good. I approve. Don't tell me you don't like her."

"Of course I like her. That's not the point."

"What is the point?"

"She'll be leaving in a few days. She's got a job offer or something in Arkansas. She's got family there."

"So? You're just going to let her go? You getting stupid in your old age?"

"Give it a rest, Mel. In the first place, it's really none of your business."

"Of course it is. I may not want you for myself anymore, but that doesn't mean I don't want to see you happy. If I hadn't been out of town when you hooked up with that what's-her-name, the piranha, I could have saved you a lot of grief."

"You didn't try to save me any grief over Connie Sue."

Melanie snorted. "Like I didn't try. You got what you deserved with that clinging vine."

"Yeah, yeah, you're all heart. But none of this has anything to do with Emily." This conversation, he thought, was getting out of hand. The toes of his boots suddenly became fascinating. He stared down at them. "It's not like that with her."

"Well, I should think not. Emily's got a brain in her head, and she's a nice lady. And she likes you."

Sloan's head shot up. "She said that?"

"Ho! That got your attention."

Sloan felt like an idiot. Mel was playing with him. He tried to remember if he'd done anything to make her mad lately, but couldn't come up with an incident that she might think required retribution. Besides, Justin was the one she usually played her practical jokes on, mainly because he played them on her. Occasionally they got together and played them on someone else.

"Okay," he said. "So she likes me. I'm a likable guy. But as soon as her car's fixed, she's gone. She's not cut out for life out here."

"Been thinking about asking her to stay, have you?"

"Of course not," he denied. "I just told you, she's not cut out for living on a ranch."

"Says who?" Melanie demanded.

"For crying out loud, her first full day here I had to haul a roast out of the oven for her. Little fool was going to try it herself, and the damn thing weighed about as much as she does. She's going to kill herself hauling that damn vacuum cleaner up and down the stairs, and she can't even fry bacon without burning herself."

Melanie stared at him, her mouth hanging open. "What did you say?"

"Aw, hell, those were just examples. From what I hear, you saw how helpless she is the other day when the washer blew a hose. If you hadn't been here we'd probably still be knee deep in water. Thanks, by the way."

"Of all the—" She swallowed the rest of her words. "In the first place, big guy, the only thing I did the other day was help her drag the washer out from the wall. It weighs slightly more than a stupid roast. It took both of us. In the space of ten minutes I saw her drag socks out of a vacuum cleaner, doctor her daughter's scraped elbow, replace a hose on the washing machine and mop down the entire porch and everything on it. Then, without batting an eye, she served me a slice of my own pie, heated and with ice cream. She never even broke a sweat. Helpless, my ass, Chisholm. You better take those blinders off or you're going to miss out on the best thing that ever happened to you.''

Sloan didn't plan on saying another word. He'd already said too much as it was. But before his brain could still his tongue, words spilled out. ''You don't know what you're talking about. She reminds me so much of my mother it terrifies me.''

''Your mother?'' Melanie shrieked. ''You really do have blinders on, don't you? It's you who's got the problem, not Emily. You just forget everything I've said and let Emily leave. She's too damn good for an idiot like you. Ask yourself this, Sloan. If she's so damn helpless, so completely wrong for you, why are you still attracted to her?''

Without another word, or letting him get one in, she whirled and stomped back to her truck. Before her dust settled, before his mind could clear out the fog that had suddenly filled it, Emily appeared before him. Just appeared, as if by magic.

''What,'' she said tightly, ''was that all about?''

Sloan's heart dropped to the pit of his stomach. ''How much did you hear?''

Emily propped her hands on her hips. ''Oh, not much. Only that you think I'm a helpless, incompetent idiot.''

''I never said—''

''I heard what you said.'' She had never been so hurt, so angry. She felt betrayed. Why, she wasn't sure. She and Sloan were nothing to each other. Nothing more than boss and employee, and actually, Rose was her boss.

"All this time," she told him, "I thought you were being so nice, such a gentleman. Offering me this job, opening doors for me, the heavy lifting, your concern over every little thing I do. I wonder if you really think I'm helpless, or if you're trying to convince me I am."

"Emily, I'm sorry. I never meant to hurt your feelings."

"My feelings? Is that what this is about? After today, I'm beginning to think maybe it's *your* feelings that are the problem here."

"What are you talking about?" He looked like a confused, whipped puppy.

Emily didn't care what he looked like. She wasn't about to let him off the hook. "Convince me I'm helpless, that I don't belong here, and I'll leave, just the way I planned to, and you won't have to deal with your feelings for me."

"What difference does it make what I think?" He didn't look so downtrodden and misused now, he looked angry. "You're leaving anyway. You make that clear every time I get near you. You've as much as said that being with me is a waste of time."

"I never said any such thing. Every time I mentioned leaving, you never suggested anything else. Because you think I'm what, too weak, too helpless? I'm not helpless, Sloan Chisholm, I'm not. I don't know who you see when you look at me, but you're not seeing me. This is me." She whipped off her shirt and tossed it over her shoulder.

''Emily! Are you crazy?'' He stepped around her and scooped up her blouse. ''Put this back on.''

''Why? So you can go on seeing me the way you want to, instead of the way I am? But then, you don't know who I am, do you?''

''The whole damn world's going to know who you are when they walk in here and see you half-naked.''

''Nobody's going to walk in here, and so what if they do?''

''Where are your girls?'' he demanded. ''Don't you care about them?''

''Of course I care. I'd die for them and you know it. It just so happens they're in their room for the next hour, and Justin is staying in the house to make sure they stay put. Your grandmother's in town and not expected back until supper, and Caleb is out riding the range, or whatever. Nobody's going to walk in here, so you can quit worrying that you'll be embarrassed.''

''I'm not worried about me, damn it. Put your clothes back on.''

''I will not,'' she shot back. ''Not as long as you have trouble seeing *me,* the real me. This is me.'' With abrupt, jerky motions, running on pure adrenaline and probably, she admitted to herself, no shortage of stupidity, she unzipped her jeans and jerked them down a couple of inches.

''Emily, stop this.''

''You see these?'' She pointed to the pale marks near her hipbone. ''These are stretch marks from having my body swell up to five times its normal size, both times I got pregnant. I carried two babies to term, gave birth to two babies, natural childbirth both times. Michael was there, holding my hand, but he sure didn't step in and finish the job for me. I was a stay-at-home mom. Do you have any idea what that means?"

"Emily, put your clothes back on."

"You think I sat around at home with my feet up all day, eating bonbons and watching soap operas? Men. What do any of you know? Do you think every time a faucet dripped, a toilet overflowed or a light switch broke, I sat down and cried and waited for the man of the house to come home and solve the problem? Do you think when Michael fell ill and I had a four-year-old and a six-year-old that I waited for somebody else to come along and help me? He was sick for two years before he died. Two long, grueling years. Grueling for him, and yes, for me, too. When he died, I buried the man I'd loved all my life. His medical expenses wiped out our finances. I had to sell the house, put the kids in day care and get a job."

"Emily, I'm sorry."

"Sorry. Prospective employers were sorry, too, that I didn't have any *real* job experience. Managing a household, raising children, nursing a dying husband, handling the finances, the plumbing, appliance repairs, none of that mattered, because I wasn't getting paid for it. It wasn't real *work.* But, no, I don't know how to pull a car engine, so I couldn't take care of that myself. That does not make me helpless or incompetent."

"I never said you were incompetent."

"You might as well have."

"Would you please put your clothes back on?"

"Why? Don't you like what you see? Or maybe

the problem is that you do like what you see, but you don't want to like it. How can you possibly be attracted to a woman you think is a helpless ninny?"

"I never called you a ninny," he cried. "Quit putting words in my mouth."

"Quit dodging the question."

"Because I can't help it!" he shouted. "All right? I can't help it. I want you."

"Despite what you think of me."

"I was wrong, okay?" Heaven help him, no woman had ever looked less like anyone's mother than Emily did in that moment. She looked like every man's secret fantasy. "You've convinced me. But even when I thought you did need help with a few things, I never thought it was your fault. I never blamed you."

"Oh, goody."

"I can't win with you," he cried.

"And I can't win with you," she fired back. "I don't know why I even want to."

Sloan lost all desire to shout. He could barely find his voice. "Do you?"

Emily wasn't ready to talk about her wants. "What did you mean about your mother?"

He closed his eyes for a moment, then turned away. "I'm not saying another word until you get dressed."

"No," she told him. "You said I remind you of her. Maybe I should take off the rest of my clothes so you can be sure I'm not her." She shoved her jeans down to her ankles, kicked off her shoes, then stepped out of the jeans.

"Damn it, Emily, what are you doing?"

"I'm waiting," she said, standing there in panties

and bra, "for you to answer my question. Why do I remind you of your mother, and what does that have to do with anything? And why should it terrify you?"

"I was wrong, okay? You've convinced me you're nothing like her. Just drop it."

"I won't drop it."

"Why not, for crying out loud?"

"Because it's important to me."

"Oh, well, that explains everything."

"I take it you thought your mother was helpless."

He let out a long breath. "She needed help a lot," he confessed.

"Like you think I do."

"She was small like you, delicate like you."

"So now I'm delicate."

Sloan couldn't help himself. He reached out and stroked her cheek. "You are. She was fragile, too, like you."

"I'm not fragile."

"To me, you are."

Emily leaned into his touch, then backed away. "What happened to your mother, Sloan."

He sighed and looked away. "She wasn't cut out for life on a ranch. It was too hard on her. Eventually, it drove her to kill herself."

"Oh, dear God. How old were you?"

"I was nine. Justin was a little thing, about two."

"I lost my parents in a car accident when I was in my teens. I can't imagine how devastating it must have been for you."

"It was roughest on our father. He blamed himself for bringing her here. Drank himself to death within two years."

Emily saw the old, deep pain in Sloan's eyes, pain he had carried all these years since losing his parents. Her own hurt feelings suddenly seemed petty. This time it was her hand that went to his cheek. "Oh, Sloan. I'm so sorry. Nothing I could say would ease the pain of your loss. But, Sloan, I am not like your mother."

He swallowed and cupped his hand over hers where it rested against his cheek. "I guess I've been wrong about you."

A tentative smile curved her lips. "I guess you have been. So, can we kiss and make up?"

"Ha. Not until you put your clothes back on."

She moved in closer to him. "You mean that I've finally worked up my nerve to make a move on you, and you're going to turn me away?"

Chapter Nine

It might have been nerves, or it might have been the combination of panic, wariness and hope in Sloan's eyes that had Emily biting back a smile.

He took a step backward, severing the physical contact. "This is kind of an about-face, isn't it?"

Emily missed the feel of his cheek against her palm, his hand holding her hand against his face. "I thought you'd be pleased."

"I am," he acknowledged. "But I'm also confused."

Emily glanced down and was sharply reminded that her clothes lay in a heap on the barn floor. She looked up again to his face, to keep from losing her nerve. "In most areas of my life I'm confident. I know what I'm doing. I'm good with my girls, and I can handle most of your average daily crises. But when it comes to my personal life, I'm not as confident. I've never had to think about having a relationship before, of being intimate with a man, because I always had Michael. I've been alone now for two years. I'm out of practice. If you don't want me anymore, just say so, and I'll go away. But if you do still want me, you're going to have to help me out, because I'm not sure how to go about this.''

Sloan was touched that she would open herself up to him so completely. He couldn't leave her twisting in the wind on her own. ''All you have to be sure about,'' he said, taking her hand and pulling her closer, ''is that this is what you want.''

She stepped closer and pressed herself against him. With her steady, blue gaze locked on his, she rose onto her toes and kissed him. A small, simple touch of lips on lips. ''I'm sure.''

He looked down at their joined hands. ''You're trembling.''

''I know.''

But she still wanted him. He could see it in her eyes, the heat, the desire. The nerves. ''Come here, then.'' He wrapped his arms around her and held her close.

Emily let out the breath she hadn't known she'd been holding. She had told him she was sure this was what she wanted. That didn't mean she was sure of *herself.* She felt that uncertainty in the chill on her skin, despite the heat of the day. When his mouth brushed hers, she sighed. Then he kissed her again, more thoroughly this time, and when his tongue swept into her mouth and touched hers, her chill disappeared.

For this space in time she would pretend that she was no longer alone. That someone strong and loving stood by her side and faced the world with her. Someone she could turn to in need, in laughter, in love. Someone she could share the girls with.

Pretending felt like heaven. Letting go of the reality of her life felt like freedom. To taste a man, to slide her hands over his chest and feel the hard muscles there, made her heart race, her blood heat, and she welcomed both the racing and the heat. His lips were soft, his body hard. The contrast was incredibly arousing.

She felt as if she were standing on a new threshold, ready to take wing and fly. Against his lips, she murmured his name.

Sloan ran his hands down her back, then up once more. "Say it again," he whispered. He had a need to hear it from her. "Say my name again."

"Sloan," she whispered. "Sloan."

Her skin felt so smooth, so soft and tender against his hard, workingman's hands, but she didn't seem to mind his calluses.

The smell of her, so sweet and womanly, contrasted sharply, for which he was eternally grateful, with the smells of clean straw and old leather that permeated the barn. The scent of flowers came from her hair, and different, softer perfume from her skin. It was enough to make a man weak.

When her breath quickened, he nearly lost his head and took her down to the floor of the barn. He wanted to take her to a soft bed, but there was no chance of that. Not this time. But he couldn't bring himself to pull away and forgo the pleasure he instinctively knew awaited them both.

He skimmed his lips over her cheeks, down along

the side of her neck. Given half a chance, he could devour her.

When his teeth grazed the tendon in the side of her neck Emily's knees nearly gave way. What kind of magic did he possess, to make her feel this way? She didn't know, didn't care, cared only that he never stop.

Then his mouth was on hers again, devouring her even as she devoured him.

His hands, hard and firm and callused on her bare skin, sent a shower of hot shivers down her spine. It wasn't fair that she couldn't return the favor. With eager fingers she attacked the snaps on his shirt then shoved the offending garment down his arms and off. Now, now she could feel his skin, and oh, it was glorious. Hot and smooth over hard muscle. Covered with hair down the center of his chest. She ran her hands over him again and again, unable to get enough of the feel of him. His sides, his chest, his arms and shoulders. His back, so broad and firm and hot to the touch.

Sloan felt every touch, every small, individual movement of her fingers. He groaned and held her tighter, walked her backward toward the stall behind him. If he didn't find something to lean against, the two of them might yet end up on the floor.

She was so perfect, fit so perfectly in his arms, against his chest. With a flick of his fingers he unhooked her bra, but he couldn't slide the straps off her arms unless she stopped touching him. He didn't want her to ever stop touching him.

She solved the problem herself and then returned her hands to his chest.

He wanted to touch her the same way, but first, ah,

first he pressed her slowly against him, her bare, soft breasts against his chest. The sensation of flesh against flesh stole his breath, made him moan. Then he was touching her, holding a firm, round breast in the palm of his hand, and again, the word *perfect* swam through his mind.

At the feel of his hand on her breast Emily's knees turned to jelly. Heat shot from her breast to her core. Wires, nerves, somewhere deep inside tightened. A new pulse started pounding, hot and heavy, down low in her body. He was killing her with pleasure, and she wanted to thank him. But that would require words, and her mouth was busy devouring his.

Had she ever felt this way before? She didn't think so. She hadn't known she was capable of feeling so much at once. The physical. The emotional. The sheer need to have him inside her. Tearing her mouth from his, she cried out and tried to get closer, closer. Closer.

"Sloan," she moaned.

"I know." His breathing was as heavy as hers. "I know."

He was moving, leading her somewhere. She didn't care where, only that he take her with him, that he fill this yawning emptiness inside her, and soon.

Sloan felt her surrender and cherished it. Had he ever had such a gift before? Had he ever cherished anything, anyone? He didn't know, couldn't think. He had to have her, had to sink himself into her and take them both someplace they'd never been before.

But she deserved better than to be taken against a stall door in the open barn, and straw, he remembered from his randy youth, had a nasty way of poking holes in skin. It was damn uncomfortable, and he wouldn't do that to Emily. His Emily.

He tore his mouth from hers.

She cried out in protest.

"Wait," he managed, his chest heaving. He yanked open the stall door and pulled her inside. There he tugged off his boots, then his jeans. The boots he tossed into a corner of the stall. His jeans, he laid out flat on the straw. Short of taking her into the house and parading her past Justin, and maybe her daughters, this was the best he could do.

Then, because he'd been away from her way too long, he pulled her close again, and pulled her down onto the makeshift bed.

Emily barely had time to take in his long, lean legs, his narrow hips and flat, muscled abdomen before she found herself lying on her back on his jeans with his weight, his solid, comforting weight covering her. She had to close her eyes to hold in all the sensations she was experiencing. His heat. The slight rasp of his chest hair against her bare breasts. The silky feel of the hair on his strong legs against her smooth ones. So many sensations, so many feelings. So much heat, along her skin, and in her racing blood.

She opened her eyes and stared up into his dark brown eyes and thought they might devour her, so hungry was their expression. That they might burn her alive, so hot was their look. Either way, devouring or burning, she could not look away.

He cupped her breast in his hand and she moaned. He flicked his tongue across her nipple and she cried out. Her hips arched against him of their own accord, but she found no argument with their effort. She wanted him there.

As his mouth settled over her breast, with tongue and teeth torturing her with pleasure, his hand slid down, down, beneath her panties and straight to the place that ached for him. When he touched her there she nearly exploded.

Sloan felt her heat, the dampness that told him she was ready to accept him. He felt her hands clutch his shoulders. Felt them slide down his back, and lower, until she was pushing his briefs down. If his heart raced any faster there would be no difference between one beat and the next.

When her legs parted, he moved between them, settling his hips there with a perfect fit, as if he'd merely been away and was now home. He eased into her slowly, *don't rush.* Slowly, to make it last. But when she opened her eyes and he looked into all that blue, he sank in to the hilt, loving the tiny gasp she made, echoing it with one of his own.

They were so in tune with each other that they started to move at the same time. Rise and fall, give and take, in and out. Slowly at first, then faster as the intensity gripped them. Faster, harder, until the rush of sensations became too much.

Emily's climax shattered her, overwhelmed her. She'd never, never felt anything so powerful in her life.

When Sloan felt her go over, felt her inner muscles clench around him, he was helpless to do anything but follow. He gave her everything he had, everything he was, and collapsed in her welcoming arms.

When he could breathe again, and think a little, Sloan raised himself onto his elbows and looked down at the woman who had just turned his world inside out. His movement made her hands slip off his shoulders. Her arms fell back, palms up, in the straw. Her eyes were closed, and she was grinning.

Sloan chuckled. "I sure do like the way you kiss and make up."

Emily felt his brief laughter through the vibrations that ran from his belly straight into hers. Heaven help her, even his laughter was arousing. How could she be aroused again after what they'd just shared?

Something unwanted niggled at the back of her mind, something she wasn't ready to face and couldn't yet name. She refused to think about it, refused to let it intrude on this glorious experience.

"As much as I like that smile on your face," Sloan said, "I think we should get dressed before we get caught." That was all they needed, he thought as he rose to his knees and pulled her until she sat before him. To get caught naked as a couple of plucked chickens by her daughters, or his grandmother. Or even worse, one of his brothers, who would tease them until doomsday.

"Ohmygod." Emily twisted left and right, jabbing her hands into the straw. "My clothes. Where are they?"

"Hey, easy. No one's coming yet. We've got time for this." He cupped her cheek, still warm and flushed, and kissed her softy. "I'm going to want to do this again, you know."

The shyness in her smile touched something deep inside of him. "So am I," she confessed.

"Maybe we can find someplace more private than the barn next time."

This time it was Emily who chuckled. "With two little girls, there's no such thing as privacy."

"We'll find a way." He kissed her again. Then, unconcerned about his own nakedness, he stood and retrieved Emily's clothes, then his own.

When they were dressed and had finished picking straw off each other, Emily turned to head for the house, but Sloan took her hand in his and drew her to a halt.

"One more," he said, pulling her to his chest and kissing her hard.

Emily's head spun. The man certainly packed a punch. "I've got to get back to the house. The girls' downtime should be about up, and Justin is probably tired of waiting for me."

"I'll go with you. I need to find out if he was able to straighten out that feed invoice."

Both of them had things to do, people waiting for them, yet neither hurried on their way to the house. They ambled slowly, reluctant to let go of this brief spell of private intimacy.

"So," he said when they were nearly at the sidewalk leading to the back door. "You can't pull a car engine, huh?"

Emily smirked. "Pull an engine, ha. I can give birth. Can you? I can change a fan belt, put in a new battery, install a new kitchen faucet, unstop a clogged toilet, bandage a skinned knee and still have dinner ready on time. What can you do?"

Sloan gnawed on the inside of his jaw. "Never mind. I concede."

When they entered the kitchen Emily checked the clock on the wall and noted that the girls still had ten minutes left on their hour of "rest." Justin was at the table eating a sandwich.

''Haven't heard a peep out of them,'' he told Emily.

''Thank you, Justin. I really appreciate it.''

Justin looked from her to Sloan and grinned. ''I just bet you do.''

Emily felt her cheeks sting. Could he see on their faces what they'd been doing? Heaven forbid. To distract him, she asked, ''Did I not feed you enough lunch?'' She motioned toward his sandwich.

''Lunch was fine, I just wanted a snack. I've got a hot date later tonight, and if I'm lucky, I'll need all the energy I can find,'' he said with a cheesy grin.

Sloan made a sound that was half grunt, half laugh. ''What's the story on the invoice?''

Justin made a face. ''Still working on it. That sorry old goat couldn't find his nose with a flashlight and a road map.''

''So what else is new?''

''What's new is his daughter finally agreed to go out with me.''

''Blaire?'' Sloan looked surprised. ''I thought she had better taste than that.''

When they started with a little good-natured bickering, Emily went to check on the girls. She found them together on the top bunk, leaning off the side and watching television, with the volume down low. That they were both on one bunk meant they were friends again. Emily was relieved.

''Can we go play outside again now?'' Libby asked. ''Pretty please?''

Emily laughed. ''I think that would be all right. Put your shoes on.''

''Yes, ma'am.''

Emily waited while they put on their shoes, then

turned off the television and followed them into the kitchen.

"There they are," Sloan said with a big smile. "Everybody okay now?"

"Yes, sir," Janie answered. "We're going back outside to play now."

Justin scooted his chair back from the table and carried his empty milk glass to the sink.

"Wait, Mr. Justin." Janie stooped and picked up a small red packet from the floor and held it out to him. "You dropped your condom."

Justin, in the process of turning away from the sink, back toward Janie when she called his name, froze in midstride, his eyes wide, his jaw dropping.

Sloan coughed, covered his mouth and turned his back, his shoulders shaking.

Emily could do nothing but gape at her eight-year-old daughter. Then a new thought intruded.

Sloan must have had the same new thought, for he turned and looked at her. Neither had to say a word. They had both just realized that they had not used a condom when they made love.

But that was for later consideration. First things first.

"Uh." Justin cleared his throat. "Thanks, Janie." With his face an interesting shade of red, he took the condom packet from Janie and stuffed it into his back pocket.

"Janie," Emily said. "How do you know what a condom is?"

Janie shrugged. "At school. All the boys carry one. They think it makes them look cool, but they're really just babies." With no apparent concern at all for the shock she'd just given her mother, Janie motioned for

Libby to follow, and they went out the door, chattering about who was going to be "it" first.

As soon their voices trailed off, Justin whooped with laughter.

Emily sank onto a chair and dropped her head with an audible *thunk* onto the table.

Sloan coughed again.

"I guess I'm outta here." Justin waggled his eyebrows. "Here's hoping I need that condom tonight."

Sloan stood in the middle of the room for a long moment, then took the chair next to Emily. "I'd laugh," he said, "but I have to apologize first."

Emily took a deep breath and let it out again before raising her head. "What do you have to apologize for?"

His serious gaze was steady on hers. "For not using a condom."

Emily gave him a half smile. "Yeah, nothing like having an eight-year-old remind you."

"Emily, I have no excuse—"

She waved away his words. "There were two of us out there in the barn. It's as much my fault as yours. But as far as the timing goes, I should be safe from getting pregnant." Dear God, let her be safe. Not that she wouldn't dearly love to have another child; she'd always wanted a big family. But not now, not when she was trying to get to Arkansas, to get her feet under her and be able to support her children. How could she do that with her head in the toilet every morning for weeks on end? Because there was no doubt in her mind that the hideous morning sickness she'd suffered with Janie and Libby would pay her another visit with the next baby she carried. Just a little gift from Mother Nature to make you value your newborn all the more for having gone through hell to bring her into the world.

Mother Nature obviously never had any children of her own and never suffered morning sickness.

"Still," Sloan said, "I should have—"

"We should have," she corrected. Then she smiled. "Or, rather, maybe we shouldn't have. But we did. Just so you'll know, I don't have any diseases."

"Neither do I." Then he shook his head. "Jeez. Snakes in the morning, and condoms in the afternoon. I guess I never realized what a parent goes through."

Emily chuckled. "Oh, you haven't seen the half of it."

After a glass of iced tea and a few awkward silences, Sloan and Emily each went back to work. He had chores to do, and she had a meal to prepare.

Emily had been torn. She had wanted him to stay, wanted to sit with him and share the quiet of the kitchen. The chances of them getting another few minutes alone in the middle of the day were slim to none.

On the other hand she was relieved when he left the house. She didn't know how to act around him now that they'd been intimate. She wanted to reach out and touch him, run her fingers through his thick, dark hair. She wanted to lean over and kiss that hard, square jaw. But she hadn't felt sure enough of herself to do either.

She'd never had to go through this awkward phase with Michael. She was out of her element with Sloan.

That unwanted *something* that had niggled the back of her mind just before they'd made love tried to push its way into her thoughts, but she refused it. She wanted time to savor their lovemaking, hold it tightly to herself lest the memories start to fade too quickly.

Who was she kidding? She would remember every second of their time together in the barn until her dying day. She'd never felt that way before.

And boom, that quick, the unwanted *something* settled heavily on her heart and announced its name. Its name was *guilt.*

She had never felt before the way she'd felt with Sloan earlier. *Not even with Michael.*

Feelings of disloyalty staggered her. She closed the cabinet door, disregarding whatever it was she'd been about to do, and eased onto a chair at the table.

It was ridiculous, of course, to feel as if she were cheating on her husband. Realistically, she had no husband. But Michael had been in her heart since childhood, nearly all the years of her life. A mere two years without him could not erase the past.

Logically, feeling guilty for making love with another man was absurd. She didn't *want* to feel guilty. She felt, oddly, that Michael would be disappointed in her for clinging to his memory instead of moving forward with her life, even to and including finding a man to share her life with. Michael would want her to move on. And she had moved on. Today was a definite move forward. She should be celebrating rather than burying her face in her hands.

She had no right to feel guilty. She certainly could not regret being with Sloan. How could she, when he had shown her what she was capable of?

That, she realized, was the problem. It felt incredibly disloyal to even think, much less acknowledge, that Sloan was a better lover, that he made her feel things she'd never felt before.

Yet, if she thought about it, it made sense. Michael had never been with any woman but her, and he was the only man, until today, she'd ever been with. Whatever they had learned, they had learned together. They had enjoyed making love with each other, but after today, Emily realized that *enjoyed* was such a pale term for what could be.

Sloan had more and varied experience than either she or Michael. Of course, she didn't know how much experience he had, but it was certainly ample as far as she was concerned.

When she realized the nature of the thoughts running through her mind, her faced heated up.

She pushed herself from the chair and turned toward the cabinet. She was not going to ease her mind and escape the sense that she was betraying Michael by sitting at the table. She had a job to do, hungry people to feed. And two little girls who were counting on her to keep her head squarely on her shoulders.

The bottom line was, she would be leaving here in a few days. She would never forget her time with Sloan, but it was a brief interlude that would soon come to a close. He hadn't asked her to stay.

Even if he did, she couldn't do it. No matter how much she might want to further explore her growing feelings for him, she had to put her daughters first. And that meant getting them to Arkansas and getting hired at the factory. Her job here would end with Earline's return, and Rose Rock, Oklahoma, wasn't exactly a hotbed of employment opportunities.

Her heart chimed in and told her that the sooner she left, the better off she would be. Both she and her girls were becoming more attached to the Cherokee Rose than was wise.

Sloan stayed away from the house for as long as he could, but when he saw Caleb heading in and Justin leaving for his date, he made a beeline for the door.

He shouldn't have left Emily the way he had. There should have been tender words, but he wasn't sure he had them. There should have been soft kisses, to make sure she didn't forget what they had just shared in the barn.

But she hadn't looked approachable, sitting beside him at the kitchen table. Not after realizing that he'd forgotten to use protection, damn his hide. And certainly not after finding out her eight-year-old daughter not only knew what a condom was, but what one looked like in its little plastic pouch. Talk about a mood breaker.

He chuckled and shook his head. It was himself he was laughing at, but what he should do was kick himself. After seeing her handle Libby's screaming incident in the garden, he couldn't believe he had ever thought Emily helpless and in need of rescuing. He'd been terrified, while Emily had been calm and collected. How did she do that?

He stepped into the utility room and headed for the bathroom there. He checked his watch and noted that he had time for a shower. He looked in the closet just outside the bathroom and found a clean change of clothes.

One whiff of himself told him he needed to make good use of the shower. When he caught himself checking his appearance in the mirror after his shower a few minutes later, he laughed. Okay, so he wanted to look good for her. Just because it wasn't like him didn't mean it was dumb. Nothing wrong with wanting to look good for a pretty lady.

Now, if he could just tuck away those heated memories of their time in the barn, he might be able to look at her in front of his family and avoid pouncing. If he tried really hard, he could possibly even get out a sensible word or two.

He put on his clean clothes, gave his hair another lick with the comb, then headed for the kitchen.

He was the last to arrive, but that didn't keep him from seeking out Emily with his eyes.

As if there were some sort of internal radar operating between them, she turned to look, found him, met his gaze. Her shy smile made his heart twist. Had a woman ever made him feel this way before? Strong and tender at the same time? He didn't think so.

Then her smile faded and something else came into her eyes, something he couldn't identify, but that might have been regret. She looked away, busying herself with a skillet on the stove.

Sloan turned abruptly away, not wanting to be caught staring at her. What had that look meant?

A moment later dinner was on the table and everyone was sitting down.

Emily busied herself helping the girls fill their plates. They didn't need her help, but she had to do something to keep from looking at Sloan. She feared that all her uncertainties would show on her face if she met his gaze again.

Sloan asked his grandmother about her trip to town, and Rose filled him in. For the life of her, Emily couldn't have said a moment later what Rose had told him. Her own thoughts of guilt and betrayal, overlaid with the pleasure and excitement she'd felt in Sloan's arms, kept whirling in her mind. She didn't come out of that fog until she heard Caleb say something about her car.

"I can't figure what happened to it," he said.

Emily blinked and looked at him across the table. "I'm sorry. I was thinking about something else. What happened to what?"

"The oil pickup tube on your car. I left it lying on the tarp under the engine, and it's gone. I'll have to order a new one. I'm sorry, Emily. It's my responsibility, so you won't have to pay for a new one, but it will take a few days to get the new part."

Days? "How many days?" she asked. If she wasn't in Fort Smith in a week and a half she would lose out on the chance at a job.

"I don't know," he confessed. "A car that old, it might be hard to find an oil pickup tube for it. I'm sorry."

Emily's mind raced. She couldn't lose that chance for the factory job. What would she do if it took too long to get the new part? If she waited until the last minute, she would be too late. But how would she get to Fort Smith without her car? She had seen no bus station in Rose Rock.

Sloan might take her, but she couldn't ask him. That would be too much, for him to drive her all the way to Arkansas. She would offer to pay him, but he wouldn't accept, she knew.

Brenda. If Emily reimbursed her cousin for gas, Brenda would come get her. But she could come only on Saturday or Sunday. Fort Smith was about three hours away, so a round-trip in one day was doable, if long.

Now that she was directly faced with the reminder of her need to get to Arkansas, Emily felt dazed. She had thought she had more time. Now she realized she did not.

She cast a brief look at Sloan, but he was looking at Caleb.

"We can get on the phone and call around in Oklahoma City," Sloan suggested.

"Yeah, I plan to start that this evening."

"If you could tell me what you find out," Emily said, "I'd appreciate it. If you can't get the part and get it installed by the end of next week, then don't rush." This was Wednesday. That gave him a week and a half. It sounded like a long time to fix a car, but she knew Caleb was only able to work on it during his spare time, of which he had little. "I'll have to call my cousin, Brenda, to come get us."

Sloan's fork clanked against his plate. He stared at her in silent shock and denial.

Her daughters were not so quiet with their objections.

"Mother, no," Janie cried.

"We can't leave," Libby said, a definite whine in her voice. "We have to stay here."

"Baby." Emily smoothed her hand over Libby's hair. "We have to get to Fort Smith so I can get that new job."

"No," she cried. "We have to stay here. Mr. Sloan won the survey."

Emily blinked. "What?"

"You can't win a survey," Janie said with a note

of superiority in her voice. To her mother, she said, "He scored the highest out of everyone."

At the foot of the table, Sloan coughed into his hand.

"What survey?" Emily asked. "What are you talking about?"

"The Daddy Survey," Libby said. "We have to stay here, 'cause Mr. Sloan has to be our new daddy."

Shock stuck Emily's tongue to the roof of her mouth. Everyone else at the table seemed to have the same problem.

Finally Emily found her voice. She looked at Sloan. "You knew about this? You took this survey?"

He pursed his lips and folded his arms across his chest. "I think this would be a good time for me to invoke my Fifth Amendment privilege."

Never had she felt such dismay. She looked back to her girls. "I thought you were taking a survey on customer satisfaction."

Janie stared down at her plate. "We did that one, too." She looked up at her mother. "That was for you. This one was for us. You're not mad, are you?"

"I...don't know," Emily said truthfully. She was shocked. She ached for her children, feeling as though she had somehow let them down, failed to provide for them in a way that would make them feel as if their family was complete. Heaven help her, what was she going to do? "After supper we'll talk about it, and you can show me this survey."

"Yes, ma'am," the girls said quietly.

Chapter Ten

How well do you like little girls?

Emily's heart clenched as she stared at the childish handwriting in the spiral-bound notebook.

The girls were in bed, as was the rest of the household. She had waited for privacy and now sat at the kitchen table, alone, reading the secret wishes of two little girls who missed their daddy. She didn't notice her own tears until one fell on the page before her. She blotted it away with the edge of her hand.

Spanking. Liver and onions. Ice cream.

"Dear God." She pressed her fingers over her mouth.

Does Santa Claus know where you live?

"My babies," she whispered. "My poor babies."

How well do you like puppies? Kittens?

Devastated, she stared at the questions. Questions of her own haunted her. What was she to do? How was she supposed to make up for their lack of a father? She had tried to be everything to them. They had never let on that they wanted a man in their lives. Surely there had been signs, but she had missed them.

They wanted a daddy. She'd known they missed Michael for a long time after he died, but during the past several months they had rarely talked about him.

Now this. "Oh, babies, what can I do?" she whispered.

A moment later she heard soft footsteps coming down the stairs. With a sniff, she wiped her face dry and closed the notebook.

"I thought you might still be up." Rose stood in the doorway, her pink robe belted loosely at the waist, her long braid uncoiled from her head and draping over one shoulder to hang to her waist. "I wanted a glass of water."

They both knew that Rose had her own bathroom upstairs. There was no need for her to come down to the kitchen to get a drink, but neither one of them mentioned that small fact.

Rose got herself a tall glass of water and sat in the chair at the end of the table. "Part of an old woman's job, it seems to me, is to poke her nose into other people's business."

Emily laughed, and realized she hadn't laughed or even smiled in hours. "Is it?"

"Of course," Rose said. "Did you find out about this survey?"

Emily flipped open the notebook. "'On a scale of one to five, with one being not at all and five being very, very much, do you believe in spanking?'"

"Oh, that's clever. They wouldn't want a new father who might spank them. You have smart daughters."

"Too smart," Emily said ruefully. "They did all this without my knowing anything about it."

"And it makes you sad, this survey?"

Emily looked down at the page of questions her babies had devised and smoothed her hand over it. "It breaks my heart."

"Because you think if you'd been a better mother, they wouldn't need anyone but you?"

Emily looked up and smiled sadly. "You're not only nosy, you're also smart."

Rose reached over and patted Emily's hand. "I raised three boys after their parents died. I know something of what you're feeling. Trust me on this, child. That your daughters want a new father is not a criticism of you. It's a tribute to the father they lost. He was a good father, wasn't he?"

"He was the best," Emily said. "He adored them, and they worshipped him."

"Which explains why they want a new father."

"I don't follow you."

"If they hadn't enjoyed having a father, they wouldn't be in a hurry to find a new one. But they loved having your husband in their lives. It was a positive experience for them, so they want to repeat it. It's the highest compliment they could pay to the father they lost."

Emily's vision blurred. She blinked to clear away the moisture. "I still feel so bad for them."

"Well, that's easily remedied." Rose took a sip of her water. When she set her glass down again, her lips curved up. "Find them a new father."

"Rose," Emily said, half laughing, half outraged.

"You don't believe it's disloyal of them to want a new father, do you?"

"Of course not."

"Would it be disloyal of you to find a new husband?"

Emily opened her mouth to speak, then shut it. This was a little too close to home as far as she was concerned.

"Ah," Rose said. "So I was right."

"About what?"

"About the way you look at my eldest grandson. The way he looks at you."

"Rose—"

"Tell me this," Rose said, interrupting. "When your second child was born, did you love your first one any less?"

"Of course not."

"There, then. Falling in love with a new man takes nothing away from what you had with your first husband. Different man, different you, different love."

"Sloan isn't in love with me," Emily protested.

Rose smiled. "If you recall, we're talking about your feelings, not his."

"I don't...I mean..." Emily shut her mouth, deciding that was the wisest course at the moment. "What about you? You never remarried?"

A faraway look came into Rose's eyes. "No, I didn't. I never found another man to tempt me after my John died."

The two women were silent for a moment, then Rose spoke. "What else did they ask on their survey?"

If someone had told her thirty minutes ago that she would be glad to read her daughters' survey, Emily would have adamantly disagreed. Now, however, she was relieved to change the subject. Gratefully she read the list of questions, and when Rose laughed at some of them, Emily found herself laughing along with her.

Rose got up from the table and carried her glass to the sink. "I'm going back to bed. You have a good night, Emily, and don't worry about Libby and Janie. They're good girls, and they're smart, and any fool can see they're happy children."

Emily stood and placed a hand on Rose's arm. "Thank you."

Upstairs, Sloan silently laughed at himself, although there was little humor in it. He wondered just how many years it had been since he'd stood in his room with his ear pressed to the door, waiting to hear his grandmother go to her room and close her door.

He'd wanted to talk to Emily earlier, but there had been no chance for privacy before she and the girls went to their room. He had hung around downstairs waiting for her to come out, but she hadn't, and Grandmother had been watching him. Outlasting him. He had given up and gone upstairs.

Then he'd heard his grandmother leave her room and go downstairs. The quiet hum of female voices drifted up the stairs, but not loud enough for him to make out what they were saying, even when he cracked open his door.

He felt like a jerk for trying to eavesdrop. He really didn't care what they were saying to each other, he just wanted to know when they were finished so he could go down and talk to Emily. He shouldn't have worried about his grandmother knowing he wanted to talk to Emily.

Definitely jerklike. He'd acted like a randy teenager earlier in the day, and now here he was, engaged in more juvenile behavior. But he couldn't put this day to rest without seeing Emily, talking to her.

He heard his grandmother's door close and waited for a count of ten, then slipped out of his room and down the stairs. He probably wasn't fooling anybody. He had visions of his grandmother and both brothers standing at their respective doors, each with an ear pressed there, snickering over his sneaking downstairs late at night to see a woman.

Well, at least if that was true, it meant he wasn't the only jerk in the house.

The living room was dark, but a light shone from the kitchen. He found Emily seated at the table. Before her lay the spiral-bound notebook Janie had used for her survey.

"They know what they want," he said.

Emily had heard someone coming and assumed it was Sloan, so the sound of his voice did not surprise her. His words, however, did. "What?"

He shrugged and leaned a shoulder against the doorjamb. "They put a lot of thought into their questions. They know what they want, how they want to be treated. Like the question about spanking. If you can get past the heartache of it, it's not only funny, it's damn clever."

"Why didn't you tell me?" Her face, her voice spoke of pain and dismay.

He straightened and strolled to the table, where he took a seat across from her. "I probably should have, but I didn't know you. For all I knew, you knew all about it."

Her eyes flew wide. "You thought I would let my daughters interview prospective fathers?"

"Like I said, I didn't know you. I didn't really think you knew what was going on, but the girls, well, hell, they trusted me. I didn't want to betray that trust. I realize that probably wasn't smart, that you needed to know what was going on. But when you came here with me I knew they couldn't do it anymore. If it helps any, I was planning to do something about it when you left here."

"Do something? You were going to tell me about it?"

He gave her a wry grin. "I knew I should, but I probably would have talked to the girls instead, told them not to survey any more men."

"Why would they need to?" She threw her hands in the air. "They've already decided you're the one. I have never been so embarrassed in my life."

He cocked his head. "Embarrassed for who?"

Emily let out a sigh. "I'm tired of thinking about this. Let's talk about something else."

"Okay." He leaned back in his chair and drummed his fingers on the table. A grin came quickly to his mouth. "Wanna pay a late-night visit to the barn with me?"

Emily groaned, rolled her eyes and dropped her forehead to the table.

"Hey," he said. "It wasn't that bad, was it?"

Emily raised her head and met his gaze. "It wasn't bad at all."

The look in her eyes sent the blood rushing from his brain to points south. Slowly he rose from his chair. ''I'm glad you liked it.'' He rounded the end of the table and stood next to her. Taking her hand in his, he tugged gently until she stood before him. ''But before we leave the subject of surveys, how are you, really?''

It took little urging, just a slight nudge to get Emily to step into his arms and lay her head on his shoulder. Did it make her weak, she wondered, to feel relief at having someone to lean on, if only for a few minutes? If so, then she was weak, and that was that. She could not bring herself to turn away from the comfort Sloan offered.

''Are you okay?'' he asked.

''I'm getting there.'' She slipped her arms around his waist. ''Your grandmother helped.''

He smoothed his hands up and down her back. ''She's good at that sort of thing.''

Emily chuckled and rubbed her cheek against his shoulder. ''With you and your brothers, I'm sure she's had a lot of practice at getting to the heart of a problem.''

His answering chuckle rumbled through her chest. ''You can say that again.''

They stood that way, their arms around each other in the silent kitchen, for a long moment. Then Sloan trailed a string of kisses from her temple to her jaw. Emily turned her head to meet his mouth with hers. The potent mixture of comfort and arousal weakened her bones. She tightened her arms around his waist and hung on, welcoming his deepening of the kiss.

In seconds her breathing was harsh, her heartbeat racing. Heat pooled between her legs. She arched her body to get closer to him. A tiny whimper escaped her throat.

The sound drove Sloan wild. He drank in the flavor of her, inhaled her scent. He wanted to gobble her up in three quick bites. There was no way he could stop himself from slipping a hand to her breast and squeezing gently.

It felt, Emily thought hazily, as if her breast swelled to fill his hand. Her whimper this time came out as a deep moan.

Sloan tore his mouth from hers and covered the side of her neck with his teeth and open mouth. "I want you."

She could feel the hard evidence of that want pressing against her. Her hips surged against him in pure reflex.

"That damn barn," he said, his breath coming in sharp gasps, "is looking better and better. We can take a blanket, and we won't have to worry about anyone walking in on us." He kissed his way back up to her mouth, where he nibbled, teasing her with the promise of more. "We can take our time."

Just the thought of what they could do together, how it would be, tempted her to grab his hand and race out the door into the night.

But responsibility and common sense reared their ugly little heads. "I can't."

"Em."

"I want to." She pulled back and held his face in her hands, forcing him to look her in the eye. "I want to. You have no idea how much I want to. But I can't go off and leave the girls."

He let out a breath and lowered his forehead to rest against hers. "I guess I knew that."

"And, Sloan?" She waited until he raised his head

and met her gaze again. "I still have to leave by next weekend."

Sloan felt as if he'd been kicked in the gut. Why, he didn't understand. They still had more than a week. He'd known from the beginning that she would soon be leaving. He had accepted that. No problem.

But that was before he had held her, kissed her, sank into her hot sweet depths and burned himself alive inside her. For a time, he'd forgotten she wasn't his.

But that wasn't right. She *was* his, no matter where she went. He knew that, felt it in his bones. Yet she would leave. She had a life to build for herself and her daughters. He couldn't fault her for that, and wouldn't try to stand in her way. That didn't mean he wouldn't grab for all she would give him while she was here.

"If you're not staying," he said solemnly, "shouldn't we make the most of what little time we have?"

Emily didn't know what to say. He was acknowledging that she would soon leave. He respected her enough to refrain from trying to interfere in her plans.

He was not asking her to stay.

Had she hoped he would? Had that faint hope lived inside her unvoiced? That couldn't be. She had risked everything, her and her daughters' futures, on this move to Arkansas. She couldn't, wouldn't turn away from it. She owed her daughters a solid future, and this was the only way she knew to provide it. The only way she could want him to interfere in that would be if she was in love with him. And of course, she wasn't.

But if she wasn't in love with him, why did it feel

as if she was tearing out her own heart when she thought of leaving him?

"Em?" He gave her a small, gentle shake.

"I have to think about it, Sloan."

"Okay," he said. "That's fair. But don't think too long. According to you, we don't have much time to spend together. Think fast, Em."

Then he gave her something to think about. He kissed her. It was long and hard and all-consuming. It left her head spinning and her heart reeling.

"Think about me," he said.

And Emily thought. About Sloan, about his kisses, his lovemaking. About her daughters. About Arkansas. She thought about leaving the Cherokee Rose, leaving Sloan. And she thought about the fact that he did not ask her to stay.

Yet hadn't he said *if* she was leaving? Did that not indicate he thought she might change her mind and stay?

But he hadn't asked her to say. Announcing that she might stay would be to assume that he would welcome such a decision. The height of presumption on her part, it seemed to her.

No, she could not stay. So was there any point in getting any closer to him, in risking her heart?

She was no closer to an answer after a sleepless night, nor when she saw Sloan at breakfast the next morning. She put a smile on her face for her daughters and for the Chisholms, and she went about her daily chores. She met the family with calm efficiency and a hearty meal when they came in at lunch, and again a few hours later when the family gathered for supper.

After she had cleaned up the kitchen for a final time that day, she turned to find Sloan standing behind her.

"Can I get you something?" she asked. "There's pie left. Would you like another slice?" She reached for a plate in the cabinet.

"No." He grasped her hand and threaded his fingers through hers. "Thank you, but no, I don't want any more pie, as good as it was."

Emily saw in his eyes the desire that she had been fighting in her own heart.

"Come for a ride with me," he said.

"A ride?"

"Back to the pond. Just the two of us."

Emily's heart started pounding. "I can't leave the girls."

"They're going to watch a Disney movie with Grandmother. They'll be glued to the TV for two hours."

"I can't take advantage of Rose that way."

"What advantage? I've already asked, and she said it was fine. Besides, it gets me off the hook. I'm grateful I'm not the one who has to watch those 101 spotted puppies again. It's her favorite movie. She's about worn out the video, and rumor is, she's got the sequel now."

"You've arranged for your grandmother to babysit my children." Was she supposed to be grateful for his thoughtfulness? Or angry at his presumption?

"Is that a problem?" he asked.

"I'll have to think about that."

"But you'll go for a ride with me?"

Emily didn't know why she was quibbling. Yes, she was leaving in barely more than a week and would surely never see him again. But, for right now, he wanted her, and she wanted him. "Yes," she said. "I'll go for a ride with you."

Sloan had tried to think of everything. He had ridden out to the pond earlier to set the stage. He had arranged for his grandmother to watch the girls. He had a quilt rolled inside a blanket strapped on behind his saddle. To prove he could be civilized as the occasion merited, he had a carefully wrapped bottle of wine and two wineglasses in his saddlebags. Candles, he had decided, would be overkill, considering it was still daylight, and he wouldn't risk setting fire to the pasture anyway. But the pink-tinged clouds riding just above the tree line on the western ridge added a nice touch, even if he couldn't take credit for arranging them.

He was nervous, he admitted. He'd made it past the first hurdle, getting Emily to come with him. He looked at her now, as she rode silently beside him. She looked so cool and calm. So damn beautiful. So delicate, although she would fire up quickly enough if he said it aloud.

What, he asked himself for the dozenth time, was he doing? He had feelings for Emily, strong ones, growing stronger by the minute. He didn't want her to leave. Not next week, not next month. But how could he ask her to stay? She had *home* and *hearth* written all over her. Marriage. And that was something he could not offer.

Maybe she was right, maybe she was strong enough for life on the ranch. Maybe he was the one who was helpless, when it came to her and her girls. He still remembered the sheer terror that had seized him when he heard Libby scream. The sharp fear of seeing Emily fall to the ground.

She had handled Libby's screaming without breaking a sweat, while his hands had shaken for more than an hour.

Maybe it wasn't her at all who was the problem, but him. In any case, a man should be in love with a woman before he asked her to marry him, and she should love him, too. That wasn't the case with him and Emily. They liked each other, cared for each other, and were definitely attracted to each other. But love? Surely not.

So where did that leave them?

He doubted there was a job available anywhere in the county that would pay her enough to support herself and her daughters, pay for a place to live, day care, clothes, food and everything else required to keep a family going.

It would be easy to suggest she simply remain as their housekeeper, but that would mean firing Earline, and that he could not do. It wasn't fair, it wasn't right, and Emily, not to mention his grandmother, would have nothing to do with such an arrangement.

That left Emily and him with few options. No options, as far as he could see, except to make the most of the short time they had left.

In all of his musings, there had been one important point in the back of his mind. He had mentioned it once to Emily, but she hadn't taken him seriously. She thought he wouldn't bother with driving to Fort Smith to see her.

The hell he wouldn't, he thought as they approached the pond. Unless she simply refused to see him after she left, he planned to do just that. There had to be more for them than these few days.

"Oh my."

Sloan heard Emily's quiet comment and knew she'd finally seen what he'd done.

"Do you like it?"

"Like it?" Emily had to blink to clear the moisture from her vision. "Sloan, it's wonderful." She couldn't believe he'd gone to so much trouble. He must have ridden for hours to gather all the bunches of wildflowers that greeted them as they rode up to the pond. She didn't know their names, but there were tiny white flowers on long stems with fernlike foliage. There were black-eyed Susans, small pink cuplike blossoms, little blue flowers on stalks of long, green grass. All of them grouped in a large arc facing the pond.

As they rode closer she realized the wildflowers were stuck in old coffee cans, Mason jars, milk jugs, whatever would hold them. And obviously, would hold water, too, or else the flowers would have long since wilted in the day's heat.

He'd done all this work for her. She was moved almost to tears by his thoughtfulness. It had been a long time since anyone had done anything special for her.

They drew their horses to a halt beneath the big willow tree and before she could swing down from the saddle, Sloan was there. With his hands around her waist, he lifted her down until she stood between him and her horse.

Then he kissed her. It was a slow, luscious melding of lips and tongue and teeth. With her legs already weak from the ride, Emily didn't have a chance of standing on her own. She leaned on him for support.

A deep tension inside Sloan dissipated when he felt her slight weight rest against him. This time he was going to take it slow and savor every moment with her, every inch of her.

He broke off the kiss and led her to the base of the willow. He turned her until she faced away from the pond. ''Stay right there.''

She turned to follow when he headed toward his horse. ''But I want to see the—''

''Just—'' He turned her around again and led her back to the tree, again facing her away from the pond. ''—stay here. You can see everything you want to see—'' he wiggled his eyebrows ''—in a minute.''

She narrowed her eyes. ''What are you up to?''

''It's a surprise. Just stay here with your back turned so I can take care of a few things. Promise?''

What was he up to now? she wondered. ''All right, but I don't need any more surprises. The flowers are beautiful.''

''I'm glad you like them.'' He placed a kiss on her forehead. ''Now behave and stay put. I'll be right back.''

Emily stayed where he left her, tracking him with her ears. She heard him lead the horses farther along the shore of the pond. She heard the creak of leather. He must be loosening the cinch on each saddle.

The grass swished with his footsteps. Then a rustling and a snap. A blanket? More swishing through the grass, then the distinctive chime of glass ringing against glass.

Her heart started racing. He had obviously gone to even more trouble than she'd first assumed. She bit back nervous laughter. Did he honestly think he needed to seduce her? She had already nearly melted in his arms.

Around her, the long narrow leaves of the willow rustled gently, while the larger rounder cottonwood leaves made a clattering sound as they slapped against each other in the slight southern breeze.

She heard again the swishing of grass, this time coming toward her. She was suddenly wound so tight that she barely avoided jumping when his hands settled on her shoulders.

"Close your eyes."

"Sloan, this isn't necessary."

"Humor me," he said. "Just close your eyes."

She did, and he wrapped an arm around her and turned her toward the pond. The ground sloped down toward the water. With the first step he encouraged her to take, she stumbled.

"Careful," he said. "Here, this is better. Keep your eyes closed."

Suddenly the ground fell away beneath her. "Sloan!"

"Hold on."

It took her a moment to realize that he had picked her up and was carrying her in his arms. "What are you doing?" It was, she admitted, a stupid question. She wrapped her arms around his neck and held on.

He stopped walking. He slipped his arm from beneath her knees and stood her on the ground. When he had her facing the direction he wanted, he stepped from behind her and stood at her side.

"Okay," he said. "You can open your eyes now."

Emily opened her eyes and gasped in surprise and pleasure. A beautiful, colorful quilt, made in the star pattern, was spread out between her and the water's edge. He had added flowers to each corner of the quilt, and at the edge nearest the water sat an open bottle of red wine and two wineglasses.

"Oh, Sloan. How lovely." She looked up at him. "Thank you."

He smiled. "Come sit down." He tugged her to the center of the quilt and sat.

When she joined him there, he began pulling off his boots. No small feat, Emily thought, no pun intended, without the use of a bootjack. Then she remembered that he had managed it well enough in the barn yesterday, so perhaps it wasn't as difficult as it looked.

Whatever, it looked like a good idea. She toed off her sneakers and set them, as Sloan did with his boots, on the grass beside the quilt, then peeled off her socks and tucked them into her shoes.

"I thought this might be nicer than the barn," he said.

Emily smiled and sipped her wine. "The air is fresher."

He let out a short laugh. "It is that. Em, you deserved better than a stall in the barn."

"You can't possibly be taking responsibility for that," she said. "If you recall, I'm the one who stripped down and came at you like a shameless hussy."

His grin was slow and devilish. "Oh, yeah, I definitely remember that. And I'll be grateful for it until my dying day." He leaned forward and kissed her.

Her mind simply shut down. She tasted rich wine on his lips and tongue. She smelled sweet clean wind and growing things.

Sloan pulled back, then tilted his head and kissed her again, a little harder this time, a little deeper. "You deserve a bed with satin sheets and candlelight. I can't give you those things right now. I'm sorry."

"Don't be," she told him. "This is wonderful. It's special and thoughtful, and I love you for it." The instant she said the words, she knew they were true. She did love him. Heaven help her.

Her words shook Sloan. She didn't mean them, of course. Not the way he wanted her to. But he would hold them close inside just the same. He kissed her again. Then again, and again.

"If you keep this up," she said, "I'm going to spill my wine and it will put an ugly stain on this beautiful quilt."

"Since I plan on keeping this up," he said, dipping in for another quick kiss, "we better figure this out."

Emily set her glass of wine on the grass, beyond the edge of the quilt. She turned back and reached for his, placing it next to hers. "What's to figure?"

"Ah." He moved in closer and nudged her until her elbows were the only things keeping her from lying down. "A woman after my own heart."

The next thing Emily realized, she was lying on her back, staring up at the blue, blue sky, with Sloan leaning over her.

Sloan knew they had all the time they wanted. There was no rush, even if they stayed until late. The horses knew the way back to the barn no matter how dark it got. Yet he felt an urgency building inside him to have her beneath him, embracing him, taking him in.

Slowly, he reminded himself. *Slowly.*

With the tip of one finger, he traced her eyebrow,

the line of her cheek, the length of her jaw. "You are so incredibly beautiful."

Her throat worked on a swallow. "You make me feel that way, when you look at me like that."

"I knew your eyes were the color of the sky before I ever saw you." He kissed each eyelid.

"How did you know such a thing?"

"Because I knew that only a beautiful, blue-eyed angel could have given birth to those two little blue-eyed angels who greeted me at the door of that café."

She smiled and ran her fingers through his hair. "You say the sweetest things."

"I try."

"You don't have to, you know."

"I don't have to try?"

"You don't have to say sweet things. You don't have to seduce me. You did that with the flowers."

He stared into her eyes, and kept staring as he kissed her. "How is a man supposed to resist you?"

"What if I don't want you to resist me?"

"I can't tell you," he said, moving toward her mouth again, "how relieved I am to hear that." He settled his lips over hers and tasted the wine, and himself, on her tongue. While he deepened the kiss, he smoothed his hand from her hip to the side of her breast.

Emily was burning from the inside out, but she didn't want to rush things. This could easily be the last time she and Sloan would be together this way. She would be gone in barely more than a week, and privacy was at a premium. They might not find another chance to be alone together. She wanted to savor every moment, to press each touch, each sensation deeply into her memory to pull out for warmth on the cold, lonely nights ahead. She would take whatever he offered, give whatever she had, and she would have the memories to last a lifetime.

She moved, trying to shift his hand to cover her breast.

"Not yet," he whispered against her mouth. "Not yet." He stroked his hand back down her side, along her hip. "You feel so good." But he wanted to feel more. He slid his hand beneath the hem of her knit top and traced his fingers back and forth across the silky skin of her abdomen. The way her muscles quivered in response sent his blood rushing.

The knit top was in his way. Pulling it off over her head was a simple matter, one which she helped him accomplish. He tossed it aside. Her soft skin, so pale next to his, fairly begged to be tasted. He pressed his open mouth where his fingers had been.

Sweet. She tasted as sweet as he'd known she would. But just to make certain, he tasted another spot, and then another, until he had tasted every inch between the waistband of her jeans and the bottom edge of her bra. Then he kissed his way up the center of her ribs, over the middle of her bra, over her chest, up her neck, until he reached her mouth.

While he feasted on her mouth, he reached beneath her and unsnapped her bra. With a slight shift of his weight, he was able to slide the straps down her arms and away. He raised onto his elbows so he could see what he'd just revealed.

"So pale," he whispered. "So perfect." With both hands, he cupped her breasts. They plumped beautifully to fill his palms. He flicked first one tip then the other with his tongue and watched them harden.

Emily sucked in a sharp breath. He was killing her,

slowly, one kiss, one breath at a time, and she welcomed it. When he brushed his tongue across her nipples she cried out at the sudden sharp sensation that arrowed from those twin points to deep in her belly.

She felt his fingers trail down her middle, then reach for the snap on her jeans, then the zipper. Her stomach muscles quivered. She helped him push down her jeans then she kicked them off.

He reared back and sat on his heels to look at her. She could feel his eyes on her as if they were his hands. It was the most erotic sensation she'd ever known, lying there, spread out before him, naked, like a feast for the taking, while he sat there fully clothed with the fire of heightened passion in his eyes.

Sloan gazed down at her and thought he'd never seen a more beautiful sight. Until she pushed him over and rose above him, her knees straddling his hips. She took his breath away.

"It's my turn now." She pulled his shirttail from his jeans and began working the buttons. When she finished she spread his shirt open and ran her hands over his chest, making his breath catch. In that moment there was nothing in the world he wouldn't have done for her. He was her willing slave.

She tugged his shirt down his arms and away, then set to work on his buckle. His snap. His zipper. She was careful with the zipper, not letting her fingers touch him at all. It nearly killed him.

She started working his jeans down over his hips, but had trouble. "Help me," she said, frustration coloring her voice.

"Gladly." He shucked his jeans and shorts and watched her face.

Her gaze started at his feet and moved up, slowly.

The smile on her face was secretive, self-satisfied. When she reached his loins, he could have sworn she actually touched him. His reaction was immediate and physical and made her smile widen.

Her eyes finally reached his face, and he let out a breath. He wanted her to make that same trail again, this time with her hands. Then her mouth. Oh, how he wanted her mouth on him.

But just then it was her eyes that held him captive. They were filled with an odd mix of innocence and ancient female knowledge. She made him feel more of a man than he had felt in his entire life. She made his chest swell, his brain stall. She made him as hard as a rock.

"The first time I saw you," she said, stroking his cheek with her gentle fingertips, "I thought you had the most compelling face I'd ever seen."

"I notice you didn't say handsome." He tried to smile, but a sudden rise of emotion nearly choked him. God help him, was he in love with her? Could that be what this soaring, trembling feeling meant?

"Handsome?" She shook her head. "Such a weak word for such a strong face. I'd never really noticed a man's looks before, until I saw you." She leaned down until the only thing separating her lips from his was a scant breath. "I'm so glad I saw you that day. So glad," she said, taking a quick nip of his lips, "that you came in for lunch."

He ran his hands up her sides, then around to capture her breasts. "Not half as glad as I am," he said with feeling.

She kissed a trail down his jaw to his neck and had him hissing in a sharp breath. He held that breath and told himself not to move as she kissed a path down his chest, along his hip. But she bypassed the part of him that throbbed in want of her.

Emily knew what he wanted, but she would wait, would make him wait. As she was waiting for what she wanted.

His skin was firm and salty on her lips. She loved the taste of him. The hair on his legs was soft and dark. His feet long and broad. And ticklish, she noted with a smile as she kissed his arch and he jerked.

On her way back up his long lean body she used her hands, feeling the bone and muscle that made up the man she loved. Would she ever touch him this way again after today?

She couldn't think about that. They were here together for now. That had to be enough. She would make it enough.

When she reached the tops of his thighs, she wrapped a hand around his erection and felt it leap in response.

Sloan thought his heart would stop when she enclosed him in that soft hand. It did stop a moment later when she swiped her tongue across the head. His hips rose from the quilt and he thrust himself hard into her hand. He didn't know how much more he could take, but he was willing to find out.

She placed open-mouthed kisses up his chest and straddled his hips again. With her gaze locked on his, she grasped him in her hand again and started to take him in. Only then did he remember.

"Wait." His voice came out as a harsh rasp. "Jeans." He reached for them. "Pocket." He fumbled until he found the red packet and tore it open.

Emily waited, on fire for him, while he put on the

condom. She couldn't believe she had forgotten about it. Again.

When the condom was in place Sloan rose up and reversed their positions, settling himself between her legs. His weight anchored her, made her feel safe and cared for. Aroused her.

Then he was pushing himself inside her. She opened herself and breathed his name. He filled her as she had never been filled before. She would swear he touched her heart. When he was inside her she felt complete and beautiful in a way she had forgotten, or maybe had never known. The beauty of it stung her eyes.

They moved together, slowly at first, give and take, in and out. She gave him everything she had, everything she was, hoping it would be enough to keep her in his mind when she was gone. She knew she would remember him and their lovemaking for the rest of her life.

Heat pooled. Points of fire licked. Nerves stretched tighter and tighter until slow was no longer an option. Faster. Harder, hotter. On and on.

Emily felt herself reaching for that peak, the top of the world, where she could hurl herself into nothingness. Closer. Almost there. Almost.

It was on her with surprising force, hurtling her off the edge of the world and sending colored lights exploding to blind her. That he followed her into oblivion so quickly, that they were so in tune with one another and could bring each other so much pleasure, brought tears to her eyes.

Sloan didn't want to come back to reality. He wanted to stay in the warm, sweet world of Emily's arms and let the real world just float on by. This had been the most incredible experience of his life. He raised himself onto his elbows to relieve her of some of his weight and looked down at her closed eyes.

He just wished he didn't have the sinking feeling that with every kiss, with every touch, she had been telling him goodbye.

He also wished, he thought wryly, that his vision would clear. Was he going blind? What had happened to the light?

A glance over his shoulder made him swear. He wanted more time. Time enough to start over and love her again as completely as it was possible for a man to love a woman. Time to savor being with her.

They weren't going to get it.

"Storm's coming in."

Emily blinked open her eyes. "I think it's already been here."

He smiled. "You are the most remarkable woman."

She smiled back and closed her eyes again. "You're not so bad yourself."

He dropped his forehead to hers. "We've got to get out of here. Damn it, this isn't how I wanted the evening to end."

"I know. Me, neither." She placed her hand on the side of his face.

Sloan turned his head and buried his lips in her palm. A deep rumble of thunder sounded in the near distance. "That storm's not going to wait. It's coming in fast and looks nasty."

"Then I guess we better go."

He would have felt better if her voice hadn't shaken.

Chapter Eleven

They raced the storm all the way home. They beat it, but just barely. It proved, according to Sloan later that night, to be the worst storm of the season. The initial gust front had winds clocked at seventy-two miles an hour. Hard, heavy rain pounded the ranch for hours as the storm front stalled, trapped between the cool dry air from Kansas to the north and warm moist air blowing up from the remnants of a tropical storm in the Gulf of Mexico.

A few minutes after Emily and Sloan had taken care of their mounts and made it to the house, the rain had come in torrents. Then had come the hail. It had viciously hammered everything under the sky. After several minutes it eased off.

The family had trooped out onto the front porch to find the ground covered in millions of small white pellets of ice about as big around as a nickel.

"We'll be checking the roofs on all the buildings in the morning for damage," Sloan said.

When the rain started up again, hard and heavy, they all went back into the house.

While the girls and the family watched television Emily divided her time between making popcorn and fresh iced tea, pacing the kitchen floor and watching the clock. Brenda had called while she and Sloan had been at the pond. She was supposed to call back at nine.

Emily looked at the clock again. It was 8:55. "Come on, come on," she muttered to the minute hand. "Move."

Time had raced while she and Sloan had been together. Now it hung motionless like thick, heavy smoke.

The minutes were crawling. What could Brenda want? It had to be about the job at the factory, and it surely couldn't be good news.

This was killing her. She had a week left on the Cherokee Rose. After today she and Sloan might not find a chance to be alone together again. The storm had cut their time together today short, and now this worry over Brenda's call was eating at the one nerve she had left.

This was not how she had wanted this evening to be.

When the phone rang she jumped as if electrocuted.

"Emily," Rose called from the living room. "Would you mind getting that? I'm sure it's for you anyway."

"No problem," she called back.

She answered the wall phone in the kitchen. Rose was right, it was Brenda.

''They've changed their hiring schedule at the factory,'' Brenda told her.

Emily's heart skipped a beat. ''What do you mean? Changed it how?''

''They've moved it up. You have to be here Wednesday if you want to get your application in the first batch.''

''Wednesday? But my car surely won't be ready by then. We're waiting on a new part and it's taking a few days.''

''What are you going to do?'' Brenda asked.

''Can you come get me?'' She had already decided she might have to call Brenda next week and ask this very thing. The timetable had just been moved ahead one week. ''I know it's a lot to ask, but I'll pay you back, I promise. I can buy the gas. You could come Saturday or Sunday.''

''Are you kidding?'' Brenda laughed. ''When I tell Tommy I'm coming to the Cherokee Rose ranch, just try keeping us away. He'll want to drive me there himself.''

''You'll come then?''

''Saturday. Is that okay?''

Emily's stomach twisted into a knot. ''Saturday is fine. I'll see you then.''

When Emily hung up the phone and turned back toward the room, Sloan was standing there. His face was a blank mask.

''You heard?'' she asked, wondering what he was thinking.

''I heard.''

"Day after tomorrow. My cousin's coming to get me."

"Why? I thought you had another week."

"The factory moved up their hiring schedule. I have to be there to put my application in by Wednesday, and Saturday is the only day Brenda can come get me."

"I could have taken you."

She shook her head and hugged herself against a sudden chill. "I couldn't ask you to do that."

"You didn't ask. I'm offering."

"Why?" she asked, her heart breaking in two. "So we can have an extra day or two? I have feelings for you, Sloan. You have to know that. The longer I stay, the harder it's going to be for me to leave."

He closed the distance between them and stood before her, out of sight of the living room, and put his hands on her shoulders. "I'm not ready to let you go."

"I don't have a choice." *Unless you offer me one.*

He pulled her gently to his chest. "I know."

Those two pieces of her heart shattered into tiny shards. She didn't know why it hurt so much. What had she expected? That he would offer her some miraculous alternative? There was no alternative, if he wasn't in love with her. If he didn't think she was strong enough for life on a ranch.

"Em." He held her tighter. His nose nestled against her temple.

Emily turned her face, and his mouth was there, waiting for hers. She met it and, for a moment, took what he offered with all the desperation she felt. Then she pulled back, determined not to make a fool of herself.

A brief fling was obviously enough for him. It was startling to realize that she wanted so much more. Of course, she would be equally shocked to realize that a brief fling would satisfy her. She'd never had a fling, brief or otherwise, in her life. She didn't think she was cut out for it.

But she'd had a fling now, and it had been brief. Yet she knew in her heart it had not been wrong. She and Sloan, they had been so right together. Even now, standing here in his arms with goodbye only a heartbeat away, he still felt right to her.

"I better go," she told him. "The girls will come looking for more popcorn any minute."

No sooner had she spoken the words than Janie stepped into the kitchen. She looked at her mother, then at Sloan, and back to her mother. "What's the matter?"

Emily forced a smile for her daughter. "Nothing, honey."

"Was that Cousin Brenda on the phone? What did she say?"

Emily hadn't planned to tell the girls just yet, because she knew they would be upset. But Janie had asked, and Emily would not lie. She told her daughter what was happening.

"Saturday?" Janie cried. "But that's day after tomorrow."

"I know, honey."

Libby joined them. "What's day after tomorrow?"

Janie looked at her mother accusingly. "Cousin Brenda's coming to get us and take us to Arkansas."

"Mommy, no! Not yet," Libby wailed.

Emily knelt before her daughters. "I know it's sooner than you want, but it can't be helped. Now, go back in there and watch the rest of your movie, okay?"

They hung their heads. "Yes, ma'am," they said in unison.

When they returned to the living room, Emily stood and turned back to Sloan.

He shook his head. "I don't know how you do it. If it was me, I'd promise them anything to chase that hangdog look from their faces."

Emily pursed her lips. "And they would have you wrapped around their little fingers in no time."

He shrugged and grinned. "I can think of worse places to be."

So could Emily. Namely, Arkansas.

When Emily put the girls to bed as soon as the second Disney movie was over, she took her shower and went to bed herself instead of joining the family in the living room. She was still awake when she heard the last of them go upstairs for the night.

Sloan was the last to go up, except for Justin, who had yet to return from his hot date. Funny how she could tell Sloan's footsteps on the stairs from those of his brothers.

She was still awake when the rain finally quit, and later when Justin came in, and three hours after that when the sky lightened near dawn. The lessening of the darkness surprised her. She had determined that it just might last forever.

Feeling hollow-headed from lack of sleep, Emily

rose and prepared to start her last full day on the Cherokee Rose.

She had breakfast well under way when the family started making their way downstairs. She had expected Sloan to be the first, but instead it was Justin.

"Good morning, sunshine."

Emily's lips twitched. It was as gray as winter outside. "I guess that means your date went well."

He waggled his eyebrows. "A gentleman never tells."

"Since when," Caleb said as he rounded the corner into the kitchen, "were you ever a gentleman?"

"Hey, I'm always a gentleman," Justin protested.

"Shame, Grandson." Rose entered the room. "I taught you better than to lie."

"Well, I'm usually a gentleman."

"Try again," said Sloan, joining them.

"Okay, okay. I was a gentleman once. I'm sure I was."

With a round of laughter, they took their seats at the table. Emily was grateful for the laughter and for Justin's protests that he was being unfairly maligned, for it took the attention off her and her impending departure.

Sloan did not ignore her, but neither did he initiate any conversation. She was grateful for that, too. This day was going to be difficult enough without starting it off with more tension than she already felt.

"I'll start checking the buildings for damage." Having finished eating, Sloan tossed his napkin on his plate and slid his chair back from the table. "You two ride out and check on the stock. I'll join you as soon as I can."

"I'll ride out with them," Rose said.

"You don't need to do that, Grandmother," Sloan objected.

She arched one dark eyebrow. "You don't need to tell me what I don't need to do, Grandson."

Sloan clenched his jaw. "Yes, ma'am," he muttered. This was getting to be a habit with him, he realized. Trying to protect the women in his life from hardship. A habit that was going to get his ears boxed if he tried it on his grandmother again.

There was no shame in a strategic retreat, he told himself as he made it out the back door. If he rushed a little faster than normal, well, that was his business, wasn't it?

When the door closed behind him, Rose eyed her other two grandsons. "And let that be a lesson to the two of you."

"What lesson would that be, Grandmother?" Justin asked with a cheeky grin.

"That would be that I'm not so old yet that I need to be coddled. You take care of your work, I'll take care of mine."

"Hey, I never said otherwise," Justin protested.

"Me, neither," Caleb said, his hands raised in innocence.

"Just be sure you don't."

Emily smiled at their byplay. Within a few minutes they were all outside following their plans for the day. She began cleaning up the kitchen and getting ready to fix breakfast for her daughters, who would be up within the hour.

''Mommy?'' Libby asked when the girls had finished eating. ''Can we go outside and play?''

Emily glanced out the window over the sink. The sun was breaking through the clouds. She looked at the puddles dotting the ground and thought of the girls' white sneakers. ''I don't know, baby, it's pretty messy out there.''

''Please, Mommy? We'll be careful.''

''Please, Mother?'' Janie added.

It would be good to have them out of the house; she planned to give the house a cleaning the likes of which it had never seen, as a farewell to the family that had welcomed them with open arms. Besides, who knew when the girls would get the chance to run and play outside again, especially in a place where she didn't have to worry about the dangers of traffic or strangers.

''All right,'' she told them. ''But try not to get too muddy, please.''

''Oh, thank you, Mommy.'' Libby hugged her hips.

''We'll be careful,'' Janie promised.

When Libby and Janie went outside, they sat on the concrete steps leading to the utility porch.

''It's my fault,'' Libby said sadly.

''What is?'' Janie asked.

''That we have to leave.''

''How can it be your fault?''

''It's because I got scared of the snake and screamed.''

''No, it's not,'' Janie protested. ''Besides, then it would be my fault, too, 'cause I made you watch that show about cobras that scared you.''

"Mommy thinks I'm too scared to stay here. That's why we have to leave."

"No, it's because of that job in Arkansas," Janie explained.

"I bet if I found that snake and showed everybody I wasn't scared of it, we'd get to stay and Mr. Sloan would get to be our daddy."

Janie shook her head. "I don't think so."

Libby looked at her older, wiser sister earnestly. "But we could try, couldn't we?"

Janie shrugged. "I don't think it will help, but I don't guess it will hurt anything, if you wanna look for the snake. As long as we don't get all muddy."

"We won't." Libby jumped to her feet. "Come on. Let's look in the garden."

All the plants in the garden were sopping wet from the rain. The girls couldn't walk down any pathway without brushing against one plant or another. They got wet in no time. But the ground in the garden had drained well, so the mud was kept to a minimum.

"Here, little snake," Libby called. "Here, Snakey, Snakey."

"I don't think they come when you call them," Janie said.

"How do you know? He ran away when I screamed, maybe he'll come if I talk nice. Come on, little snake, I won't hurt you."

"That sounds really silly."

"Look!" Libby pointed to a bean bush whose lower leaves, which rested on the ground, rustled. "It's him, I know it."

Janie would have expressed her doubt, but just then

a small gray snake slithered out from beneath the bush, across the path and into the tomato plants.

"There he goes!" Unmindful of the wet plants, or their delicacy, Libby charged through the bush tomatoes, and the chase was on. They followed the snake as it raced from one row to the next, until it was through the chain-link fence and out of the garden.

"Oh, no!" Libby yelled. "He's heading for the creek!"

The girls ran back out through the garden gate and followed the six-inch gray snake. Libby saw it disappear into a clump of grass near the tire swing.

"There he goes," Janie said.

"I saw, I saw." Libby slowed and tiptoed toward the clump of grass, two feet from the bank of the creek.

"Don't get too close to the edge," Janie warned.

Libby looked over at the rushing water that was nearly to the top of the banks, when usually it was five feet lower. "Golly," she said. "Look at all that water."

"Be careful," Janie warned.

"I am." She inched another step forward, and the ground, weakened and saturated by the torrential rains, simply gave way beneath her feet. One minute Libby was standing there, the next she was gone.

"Libby!"

Emily was working upstairs, giving Rose's bedroom a final going-over with the polishing cloth. The house was quiet, quieter than usual with the girls outside.

A shrill scream from outside broke the silence.

Emily's heart stopped. That was Libby's voice.

She raced to the window that overlooked the backyard, but before she reached it she heard Janie scream Libby's name.

She reached the window and threw aside the curtains to see Janie dancing back and forth anxiously at the edge of the creek, only the edge of the creek didn't seem to be where it should be.

Emily dropped her polishing cloth and tore out of the bedroom and down the stairs. She was outside in five seconds flat and running for all she was worth toward the creek.

Sloan was on the roof of the barn fixing a leak when he heard the screams. His heart jumped to his throat and threatened to cut off his air. He had hoped to never again hear the sound of a little girl screaming in fear for as long as he lived, but there it was. It was Libby, he knew. But this time her scream sounded even more terrified than the day she'd been afraid of the snake.

Then Janie screamed her sister's name.

He dropped his hammer and slid down the slope of the roof to the edge. No fireman had ever slid down a pole faster than Sloan made it down the ladder. Then he was off and running.

He saw Emily fly out of the house thirty yards ahead of him and run for the creek.

Emily raced up to Janie, who was jumping up and down in anxiety and staring down the creek. "Hold on, Libby!"

"Janie!"

"Mama! Mama, the ground fell into the creek and took Libby with it."

Terror clutched at Emily's throat. She could plainly see where the raging water had gouged out a huge chunk of ground. "Where is she?"

"There." She pointed downstream.

"Where? I don't see her."

"There, on that tree."

Emily followed the direction Janie pointed. There, on a tree branch that hung low over the water, a spot of color. "Libby!"

Her baby was hanging on to the branch with her tiny hands, while the force of the water did its best to tear her loose. The rain-swollen creek, normally barely ankle deep but now at least five feet deep, shot broken branches, large and small, directly at the terrified child.

"Hang on, Libby, Mommy's coming!"

"What are you going to do?" Janie cried.

Emily spun and grabbed Janie by the shoulders. "I'm going after her. You go find help. Sloan might—" She broke off when she spotted Sloan running full speed toward them. "Never mind. Just stay away from the creek. Stay way back."

Then Emily did the exact opposite. She raced along the bank and got as close to Libby as possible. Holding on to the same branch that was Libby's lifeline, Emily stepped into the rushing water.

The force of the water knocked her legs from beneath her, but there was nothing to stand on anyway, as the bottom of the creek was a good five feet down. The frigid water took her breath, the swiftness took her under. She held on to the thick, sturdy branch for all she was worth, tearing the skin on her palms, to keep from being washed away. The force of the water pulled on her so hard she feared her shoulders might be dislocated.

The pain centered her. The pain, and the faint cry from Libby.

"Mommy!"

With a strength she didn't know she possessed, Emily gripped the branch tighter and pulled until her head was above water. Coughing and choking, she tried to draw in air.

"Mommy," Libby cried again with terror in her tiny voice.

"Hang on, baby. Just hang on," Emily yelled over the roaring of the raging water.

Hand over hand, Emily inched her way toward her baby, praying as she had never prayed before.

"Mommy, I'm slipping!"

"Hold on, baby! Hold on tight, I'm almost there!" What she would do once she reached Libby, she didn't know. There was still nothing beneath her feet but rushing water. Nothing to stand on.

Something slammed into her leg hard enough to force a cry from her lips and blacken her vision. She shook her head, trying to clear it.

"Emily!"

Sloan! The sound of his voice gave her strength. Her vision cleared and she made it the final three feet down the branch to Libby.

The branch dipped and swayed. Emily's added weight was more than it wanted to bear. Libby screamed.

"It's all right, baby, just hold on, be still. I've got

you.'' With a deep breath and another prayer, she let go of the branch with one hand and wrapped that arm around Libby's waist. ''I've got you.''

Libby turned loose of the branch and threw her arms around Emily's neck, nearly strangling her, nearly causing Emily to lose her tentative, one-handed hold on the branch.

On the bank, Sloan nearly had a heart attack. Emily couldn't hold on much longer, not with Libby's weight added to hers, and her grip slipping on the thick branch, and the branch dipping lower and lower toward the water. She would never be able to make her way back to the bank.

In that instant Sloan had a stark glimpse of what his life would be like in the future without Emily. The sky would always be gray, the waters always dark and deadly. There would be no precious blue-eyed girls, no beautiful, yellow-haired woman. There would be only one unending, lonely night after empty day. Life without Emily, Janie and Libby, would be colorless. Hopeless. Empty.

He swore a blue streak at himself for wasting time feeling sorry for himself while Emily was fighting for her life. He searched the bank and the water for a loose branch thick enough and long enough to extend toward them so he could pull them in. There was nothing usable. With another curse, he whipped off his belt, then buckled it to make the largest loop possible. He found a place on the tree where a large branch had broken off, leaving a six-inch stub pointing up and out from the trunk. He stuck the looped belt over the stub and gripped the opposite side of the loop tightly.

"Can you get them?" Janie asked.

"I can get them. Get back, honey. I don't trust this bank, and we don't want you ending up in there, too."

Janie swallowed and moved back, terrified for her mother and little sister, but knowing that Mr. Sloan could save them. Mr. Sloan could do anything. He'd made her mother laugh and smile again, hadn't he?

Unaware of his hero status in Janie's eyes, Sloan focused on Emily and Libby. Holding on to the belt, he gave it a sharp tug, then another, testing its strength and the strength of the branch stub that held it. Both seemed sound enough.

"Hold on," he called. Then he stepped down the bank and into the foaming red water. He dug his heels into the side of the bank, fighting the strength of the current racing downstream. He leaned as far out as he could and stretched out his arm.

Too far. Emily and Libby were too far to reach.

Emily saw the problem instantly. "Wait there," she called. "We'll come to you."

"Be careful!"

"Libby, baby, you hang on to me. I'm going to take my arm from around you so I can hold on to the branch with both hands."

"No, Mommy, noo! Don't let go of me!"

"I have to, baby, but it'll be okay. See Mr. Sloan? He's waiting for us. You hold on to me, and I'll move us down this branch toward Sloan, and he'll get you out of the water. Okay?"

Too scared to cry, Libby nodded jerkily. "Okay, Mommy." She tightened her hold on Emily's neck, nearly strangling her again. But this time Emily let her. She took her arm from around Libby's back and grabbed the branch over her head.

Slowly and painfully she moved, hand over hand, toward the bank and Sloan.

"A little farther," Sloan called. "A little farther. What are you doing?"

"I'm turning around," she yelled, "so you can get Libby."

Sloan wanted to argue that he could get them both at once, but he shut his mouth. That was a fool's idea. She was right and he knew it. He could get Libby first, then Emily. It would be safer that way, as long as Emily could hold on.

"Look!"

Distracted by Janie's cry, Sloan glanced upstream. A large tree limb that branched off in a half dozen places was racing directly for Emily and Libby.

"Hurry!" he yelled. He stretched his arm out as far as he could. "Hurry, Emily."

A slap of water hit her in the face. Sputtering, she felt her hands slipping. "Hold on, Libby. Almost there. Can you get her?"

"A little farther. A few more inches. You can do it."

Her arms and hands screaming in pain, Emily inched her way up the branch. Finally she had Libby within Sloan's reach.

Sloan tried to grab the back of Libby's shirt, but it stretched so much that she would slip right out of it if he lifted her that way. Panting with effort, he forced his arm between Libby and Emily.

"Let go of Mommy, Lib," he said.

"Nooo!"

"Come on, baby, I've got you."

"Let go, Libby," Emily encouraged. "Sloan's got you. He won't let you go."

Libby's pupils were tiny pinpricks of terror. "O-okay."

The instant her arms loosened, Sloan scooped her to his chest. "There, I've got you."

Holding her in one arm, he used the belt to help him climb up the bank. "Janie, get her back from here. I'm going after your mother."

"Hurry!"

With Libby safely out of harm's way, Emily used what was left of her strength to pull herself toward the bank.

"Look out!" Janie screamed.

Emily glanced upstream. A giant limb with multiple branches was almost upon her. It would knock her hold loose and take her under. She had seconds, at the most.

"Em!"

She moved her right hand forward, then her left. Then she was out of time. She let go of the branch and threw herself forward with the last of her strength.

It was enough. Sloan caught her and crushed her to his chest. "Thank God," he managed.

By the time they crawled to shore all Emily could do was sprawl on her face in the mud.

"Mommy!"

"Mother!"

"Em?"

The three voices she loved most in the world gave her the strength to push herself up until she could sit.

Before she could draw a full breath Sloan had his arms around her and held her so tightly she feared for her ribs.

"I thought I was going to lose you. God, Em, you can't leave me. You can't."

Janie and Libby flung themselves at their mother. Sloan took them all into his arms.

"Sloan."

"You saved us, Mr. Sloan," Libby said. "You saved us from the creek."

"Are you okay?" he demanded of both of them. "Are you hurt? Libby? Em?"

"I'm fine," Emily said. "Libby?"

"I'm okay, Mommy. I was just standing there, and the ground fell in. I'm sorry."

"It's okay, baby." Emily kissed the forehead of her youngest daughter. "Are you okay?" she asked Janie.

"I'm okay, Mother. Did you hear Mr. Sloan? He said we couldn't leave."

"He's just relieved that we're all okay," Emily assured her, while her heart beat in double time.

"Yes," he said, "I'm relieved you're all okay. But I meant it, Em. When I saw you in the water, I had a terrible flash of what my life will be like if you leave me, and it's too empty to think about. You have to stay."

"Stay? What do you mean?"

"I'm saying this all wrong. You deserve candle-light and soft music, but at least I'm on my knees. That's gotta count for something."

Emily's heart hit triple time. "What are you saying?"

"I'm asking you to marry me. I want you to marry me and live here on this ranch with me and let me be a father to your daughters."

The roar of the raging creek was drowned out by the roar of her blood in her ears. "Marry you?"

"You have to, you know," he said. "I scored the highest on the survey. That means you have to marry me."

"I do?"

"Those are the right words, the minute we're in front of a preacher."

"Sloan, why should I marry you?"

Sloan gulped. He looked her in the eye and felt new strength surge through him. "Because I love you. I love all of you so much."

With a glad cry, Emily threw her arms around his neck and kissed him. He kissed her back. It was something the girls were going to have to get used to, seeing him kiss their mother. He planned to do a lot of it during the next fifty or sixty years.

Libby and Janie looked at each other and grinned.

"Does this mean we're staying?" Janie asked.

Emily pulled back from kissing Sloan and looked at the eager expressions on her daughters' faces. "Yes. We're staying."

"And Mr. Sloan's going to be our new daddy?" They looked at him.

"If you'll have me," he said.

Janie and Libby cheered and threw their arms around his neck.

Emily watched the three people she loved most in the world with a wide smile and blurred vision.

Then Sloan set the girls aside. "Can you go to the

house and get cleaned up while I talk to your mother?''

''Okay.'' The girls held hands and raced toward the house, giggling and cheering all the way.

''Oh, God, Sloan.'' She leaned her shoulder against his chest. ''I've never seen them so happy.''

''You've never seen me so happy, either, because I've never been this happy. I love you, Em.''

She turned her face toward his. ''I love you, too.''

''I was hoping you'd say that. I'm going to want to hear it a lot.''

''I'm going to want to say it a lot. I love you. I love you.''

He took her words, and then her breath, when he covered her mouth with his. They knelt in the mud along the bank of the creek that had nearly separated them forever and made promises with that kiss, promises of love and laughter and companionship until the day they died.

Chapter Twelve

Excitement fairly bubbled around the dinner table that night. Nobody had time to dwell on Libby's near drowning, least of all, Libby. Her and Emily's scrapes and bruises had been seen to, Janie praised for getting help, Sloan for his dramatic rescue.

But all of that was nothing. Libby and Janie were getting a new daddy! Sloan and Emily were getting married!

At the head of the table, Rose looked happy enough to burst. Her eldest grandson—the firstborn of her firstborn—was going to marry a lovely woman. Rose was about to gain not only a granddaughter-in-law, but two beautiful great-granddaughters, as well. She couldn't have been more pleased.

At her left, Caleb looked as satisfied as if he had already polished off the entire peach cobbler that his soon-to-be sister-in-law had made for dessert. Of course, he wouldn't get to eat the whole thing, but that was okay. Sloan was marrying the cook, so there would be more where that cobbler came from. And, aside from the fact that he loved her cooking, Caleb couldn't have picked a more perfect woman for his big brother to marry. He was about to become a brother-in-law, and an uncle, to boot. Oh, yes, life was indeed satisfying.

To Caleb's left, Justin looked—and felt, he admitted—smug. After all, he'd had the biggest hand in getting Sloan and Emily together. If he didn't count the flood. Or the girls. Or the missing car part. He, after all, had baby-sat, hadn't he?

Emily sat across from Justin, with Sloan between them at the foot of the table. Sloan and Emily looked...at each other. They couldn't seem to stop, couldn't get enough of each other. But when the girls, seated between Emily and Rose, started to giggle, Emily finally managed to tear her gaze from Sloan's, and he from hers.

When she glanced at her daughters, she frowned. They might be giggling, but something else was going on. There were nerves behind those giggles and in those eyes.

"Is something wrong?" she asked them quietly.

Janie and Libby shared a look. They both swallowed, eyes big, and looked back at their mother.

"What is it?" Emily asked with a puzzled smile.

"You're not..." Janie began, then paused.

"Go on." Libby elbowed her sister. "Ask her."

"Ask me what?" Emily wanted to know. "Come on, out with it."

Janie cast a final glance at Libby, then licked her

lips. "You're not going to marry Sloan just because our car can't get fixed, are you?"

"What?"

"I mean, you'd marry him even if our car was fixed, wouldn't you?"

"Of course I would, honey. This has nothing to do with our car. Sloan and I are getting married, and that's that. I thought you were happy about it."

"We are!" Libby cried. "We're *real* happy, aren't we, Janie?"

"*Real* happy," Janie confirmed. "We get a new daddy." She grinned at Sloan. "And we get a great-grandmother."

"You sure do," Rose told them with a big smile.

"And we get uncles." Janie looked pointedly at a beaming Caleb and Justin.

Justin leaned back in his chair and stuck out his chest. "Hear that, Caleb? We're gonna be uncles."

"Yeah. Pretty cool," Caleb decided.

Then Janie frowned. "Do you know how to be uncles?"

The two men frowned and shared a brief look.

"Well," Caleb said. "I guess we can figure it out as we go. Unless you want to give us a few pointers."

Libby nodded. "Give 'em pointers, Janie. Tell them the rules."

Justin chuckled. "There are rules for uncles?"

"Oh, yes." Janie nodded vigorously. "Uncles are like playmates, only they're already grown-up. They play with you and take you places and let you do things your parents wouldn't let you do."

Emily pursed her lips, wondering what else was coming, because after a speech like that, there was certain to be a bombshell.

"And they always take your side," Janie added.

The two prospective uncles scrunched up their faces in thought, looked at each other, then nodded.

"Yep," Justin said. "That sounds about right to me."

"We can do that," Caleb said.

Libby leaned over and whispered to Janie. "They gotta promise."

"You promise?" Janie asked earnestly.

"Cross my heart," Justin said.

"We promise," Caleb said solemnly.

The two girls looked at each other, but they didn't grin. Here it came, Emily thought. Whatever it was.

"Okay, then." Janie reached beneath the table, pulled out a long skinny tube and held it across the table toward Caleb. "Then I guess you might want this."

At the foot of the table Sloan choked on a sip of iced tea.

Next to him, Justin pressed his knuckles over lips that wanted to curve up.

Caleb blinked. "Well." He blinked again. "You found the missing oil pickup tube." Another blink, and what might have been a twitch of his lips, a sharp sideways glance at Justin. "Thank you," he said to Janie. "Where did you find it?"

Emily gaped. "That's the part that disappeared?"

"We found it on the tarp, underneath the car," Janie said in a rush.

"You did?" Caleb took the tube and studied it, shaking his head. "Must have been there all along and I just overlooked it." He cut another look at Justin, this one promising a reckoning. Caleb knew his younger brother. This thing had the kid's fingerprints all over it, figuratively if not literally. "Thanks, Janie. I'm glad you found it."

Janie and Libby looked at each other and let out a long breath of relief.

Janie grinned across the table. "You're welcome, Uncle Caleb."

Caleb beamed back at her.

"Young ladies," Emily said in her mother voice. "I think—"

Justin cut her off. "I think that's just great, the way you girls found that missing part. After supper Caleb and I can show you where it goes. We'll make mechanics out of the pair of you yet."

Libby giggled. "You're gonna be a good uncle, Uncle Justin."

He winked at her. "I'm gonna be the best."

"Now, hold on," Caleb protested. "I'm older than you. I get to be the best uncle."

Sloan rolled his eyes. "Lord, help us. I think you've just lost control of your daughters, Em. Their new uncles are going to take over."

"Not to worry," Rose said cheerfully. "No one spoils little girls like a great-grandmother. You just leave everything to me."

Sloan narrowed his eyes at his grandmother. "I know you. I know what you're thinking. You are *not* going to buy them each a horse."

"A horse?" Janie and Libby squealed together. "We get a horse?"

Emily rolled her eyes. "Now you've done it," she muttered.

"Of course you do, dears," Rose said to the girls, her eyes narrowed at her eldest grandson.

''Of course you do,'' Sloan said. ''But *I'm* getting them for you.'' He jabbed a thumb at his own chest.

''We get horses!''

Emily looked across the table at Caleb and Justin. ''Help.''

They just grinned at her. ''Welcome to the family, sister.''

Sudden tears blurred Emily's vision. ''Oh.'' She pressed her fingers to her lips. In all the excitement it hadn't really dawned on her. Yes, she was getting married—that alone took her breath away. Her daughters were getting a new father, a great-grandmother and two uncles. But it hadn't sunk in that Emily herself was getting brothers. She'd never had siblings. Now she would have brothers. Two of them.

''Em?'' Sloan took her hand in his. ''Em, what's wrong?''

Her smile might have wobbled, but it came straight from her heart. ''I love you.''

Someday she hoped to make him understand just how grateful she was. Not only was he giving her himself, but an entire family, as well.

Thank you, her heart sang.

Epilogue

Five weeks later Emily Nelson married Sloan Chisholm at the Rose Rock Baptist church in what was to have been a small intimate ceremony. Nearly fifty people showed up.

Brenda and Tommy drove in from Fort Smith. That was the extent of Emily's contribution to the guest list. Everyone else had come for Sloan.

Emily had known that Sloan had a lot of friends—she had met a few of them. She and Melanie had even become friends in recent weeks. But Emily had had no idea about the Chisholm relatives. Aunts and uncles and cousins came from all over the country. Farmers and ranchers, doctors and soldiers, and a few she was just as glad not to know about.

The groom, all agreed, was a handsome devil in his black tux, his head held high with pride. His brothers, serving as his groomsmen, were no slouches, either.

The bride wore an off-white dress that fell in graceful folds to her ankles. Everyone agreed that she glowed with a special beauty. But it was her bridesmaids dressed in pink who stole the show. Libby and Janie were full of their own importance, excited at taking part in their mother's wedding and absolutely adorable.

They stood beside their mother and stared at her, and at Sloan, in wonder, their young minds not sure what to make of all the fuss, but understanding that it might be the most important thing that had ever happened in their lives.

Their mother was marrying Mr. Sloan. He'd been the best daddy candidate they had found, and, as far as they were concerned, he was wonderful.

To Janie's mind, they had stated their goal—a new father. They had made a plan and surveyed every man they met. In the end, it was a matter of adding up the numbers, totalling the scores. Everything logical, sensible. If you kept things sensible, you could have what you wanted.

Libby looked at things differently. To her this wedding was proof that if you squeezed your eyes shut tight enough and wished hard enough, good things happened.

They had argued about their opposite views and decided that maybe, just maybe, they were both right.

When the *I-dos* were said and the groom kissed his bride, Libby and Janie shared a look.

''Now?'' Libby whispered, her eyes alight with excitement.

''No.'' Janie shook her head and held on to her sister's arm. ''We have to ask first.''

The instant the kiss was over, as the newlyweds

turned to face their guests, Libby tugged on her mother's dress.

Misty-eyed, with her heart full to bursting, Emily turned to her daughters.

"Mama," Libby asked, "is Mr. Sloan our daddy now?"

Emily shared a look with Sloan, then touched a hand to each daughter's cheek. "That's right. Sloan is your new daddy now."

"Does that mean we don't have to call him Mr. Sloan anymore?" Janie asked.

Several guests in the front rows chuckled.

"No," Emily said. "You don't have to call him Mr. Sloan anymore."

Sloan slipped his arm around Emily's waist and smiled at his new daughters. "So, what are you going to call me?"

Janie and Libby moved to stand before Sloan and looked up at him. "If it's okay," Janie said, taking her sister's hand in hers and squeezing, "I mean, if you don't mind..."

Sloan's heart started pounding. "What is it you want to call me?"

Libby stepped up and craned her neck to look up at him. "Can we call you Daddy?"

For an instant, Sloan's heart stopped, his vision blurred. The next thing he knew, he was on his knees, hugging his new daughters to his chest. He looked up helplessly at Emily.

Emily's own vision blurred. She gave him a wobbly smile.

"I'd be honored," he said in a voice that shook, "to have you call me Daddy."

Then all he could do was mouth the words *thank*

you to Emily. Someday he hoped he could make her understand just how grateful he was that she had come into his life. For, not only had she given him herself, she had given him two precious daughters. He prayed that he could fill the shoes Michael Nelson had left and be the type of father these girls needed to see them through childhood, through the awkward teen years and on into womanhood.

But, for now, they were little girls, and they were his. And so was their mother.

Life, he decided, could not be better.

* * * * *

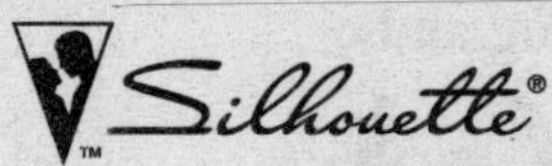

SPECIAL EDITION®

COMING NEXT MONTH

#1621 ROMANCING THE ENEMY—Laurie Paige
The Parks Empire
Nursery school teacher Sara Carlton wanted to uncover the truth surrounding her father's mysterious death years ago, but when she met Cade Parks, the sexy son of the suspected murderer, she couldn't help but expose her heart. Could she shed the shadow of the past and give her love to the enemy?

#1622 HER TEXAS RANGER—Stella Bagwell
Men of the West
When summoned to solve a murder in his hometown, ruggedly handsome Ranger Seth Ketchum stumbled upon high school crush Corrina Dawson. She'd always secretly had her eye on him, too. Then all signs pointed to her father's guilt and suddenly she had to choose one man in her life over the other....

#1623 BABIES IN THE BARGAIN—Victoria Pade
Northbridge Nuptials
After Kira Wentworth's sister was killed, she insisted on taking care of the twin girls left behind. But when she and her sister's husband, Cutty Grant, felt an instant attraction, Kira found herself bargaining for more than just the babies!

#1624 PRODIGAL PRINCE CHARMING—Christine Flynn
The Kendricks of Camelot
Could fairy tales really come true? After wealthy playboy Cord Kendrick destroyed Madison O'Malley's catering truck, he knew he'd have to offer more than money if he wanted to charm his way toward a happy ending. But could he win the heart of his Cinderella without bringing scandal to her door?

#1625 A FOREVER FAMILY—Mary J. Forbes
Suddenly thrust into taking care of his orphaned niece and the family farm, Dr. Michael Rowan needed a helping hand. Luckily his only applicant was kind and loving Shanna McCoy. Close quarters bred a close connection, but only the unexpected could turn these three into a family.

#1626 THE OTHER BROTHER—Janis Reams Hudson
Men of the Cherokee Rose
While growing up, Melanie Pruitt had always been in love with Sloan Chisholm. But when she attended his wedding years later, it was his sexy younger brother Caleb who caught her attention. Both unleashed their passion, then quickly curbed it for the sake of friendship—until Melanie realized that she didn't need another friend, but something more....

SSECNM0604